Previou

When eccentric Uncle Patrick gave Freddie an ancient map of the world, Freddie was intrigued by the unusual gift, and his uncle's cryptic message about the importance of the poem, 'If—'. Little did he know that the mysterious map was about to turn his world upside down!

Mounted on his bedroom wall, the antique map bristled with untold secrets – ones it seemed eager to share with Freddie. One minute he was in his bedroom, and the next the map had sucked him into a wildly spinning vortex where myriad portals beckoned Freddie into other lands and times. Already he had been transported to critical moments in history with urgent missions to complete first in Nepal, then in Ancient Egypt.

Encountering adversaries at every turn, hounded by a mysterious enemy, and never really knowing when – or if – he'll be able to get home, Freddie's chances of fulfilling the missions on which the map takes him seem slim at best.

But Freddie Malone doesn't give up easily. And now the map is beginning to ripple with life once again...

A FREDDIE MALONE ADVENTURE

IN THE CITY OF FORTUNE AND FLAMES

CLIVE MANTLE

AWARD PUBLICATIONS LIMITED

To find out more about the adventures
of Freddie Malone, please visit:

www.freddiemalone.com
www.clivemantle.com
f *@theadventuresoffreddiemalone*

ISBN 978-1-78270-424-9

Text copyright © 2020 Clive Mantle
This edition copyright © Award Publications Limited

Cover design and illustration by Patrick Knowles
Map, text illustrations and portrait of Samuel Pepys by Angela Hewitt
Other photographs and illustrations: Carl Sloan/Shutterstock.com (cover),
More Vector/Shutterstock.com (p281)

First published by Award Publications Limited 2020

Published by Award Publications Limited,
The Old Riding School, Welbeck,
Worksop, S80 3LR

www.awardpublications.co.uk

20 1

Printed in the United Kingdom

**For Harry, Carla,
Keith and Richard Mantle
and Martin Bashir**

If—

If you can keep your head when all about you
  Are losing theirs and blaming it on you,
If you can trust yourself when all men doubt you,
  But make allowance for their doubting too;
If you can wait and not be tired by waiting,
  Or being lied about, don't deal in lies,
Or being hated, don't give way to hating,
  And yet don't look too good, nor talk too wise:

If you can dream – and not make dreams your master;
  If you can think – and not make thoughts your aim;
If you can meet with Triumph and Disaster
  And treat those two imposters just the same;
If you can bear to hear the truth you've spoken
  Twisted by knaves to make a trap for fools,
Or watch the things you gave your life to, broken,
  And stoop and build 'em up with worn-out tools:

If you can make one heap of all your winnings
And risk it on one turn of pitch-and-toss,
And lose, and start again at your beginnings
And never breathe a word about your loss;
If you can force your heart and nerve and sinew
To serve your turn long after they are gone,
And so hold on when there is nothing in you
Except the will which says to them: "Hold on!"

If you can talk with crowds and keep your virtue,
Or walk with Kings – nor lose the common touch,
If neither foes nor loving friends can hurt you,
If all men count with you, but none too much;
If you can fill the unforgiving minute
With sixty seconds' worth of distance run,
Yours is the Earth and everything that's in it,
And—which is more—you'll be a Man, my son!

Rudyard Kipling, 1895

In the City of Fortune and Flames

Prologue

In a filthy and overcrowded city, over 350 years ago, an important and ambitious young man sat in his library writing his secret journal in a coded language only he understood.

And elsewhere, in a dark and musty basement, thousands of miles and hundreds of years away from the ambitious young man, a shrouded figure descended a flight of stairs and flicked on a single light, illuminating his deeply lined features. He removed his dark cloak and cast it over the seat behind an old desk, disturbing a blanket of dust which danced in the dimly lit room, creating the illusion of a dark and sinister snow globe.

The Collector surveyed his underground museum, full of stolen relics from throughout history. He smiled and said out loud, "Everyone should keep a diary, don't you agree?" as if telling the first line of a joke. "And I intend to keep a very famous diary. Yes indeed! I'll keep it all to myself."

He enjoyed his treasures, lovingly talking to each item in turn, and re-living the escapades involved in obtaining them. He spent less time amongst them than he'd like, because the swirling vortex that brought him here was under someone else's control now. Someone who was proving a troublesome thorn in his side.

All that was about to change. The Collector planned to lure his foe into a terrible trap and end his meddling for ever. A villainous contact of his was going to undertake his next quest, and dispose of his adversary at the same time.

"Perfect," he whispered, almost trembling with excitement. The moment had arrived to steal his next prize, and finish his enemy for good.

It was all just a matter of time.

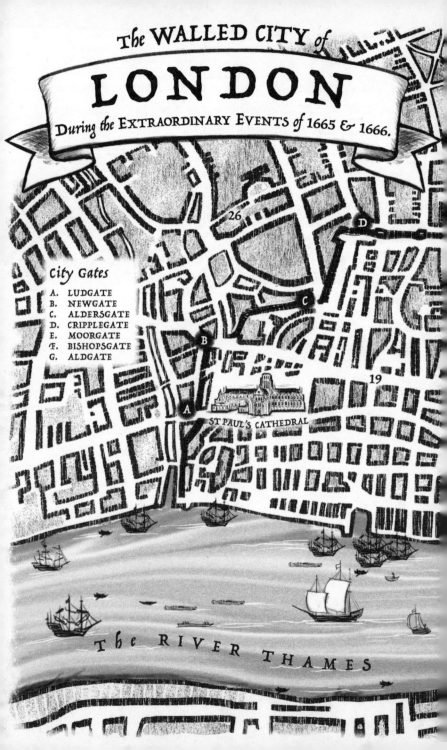

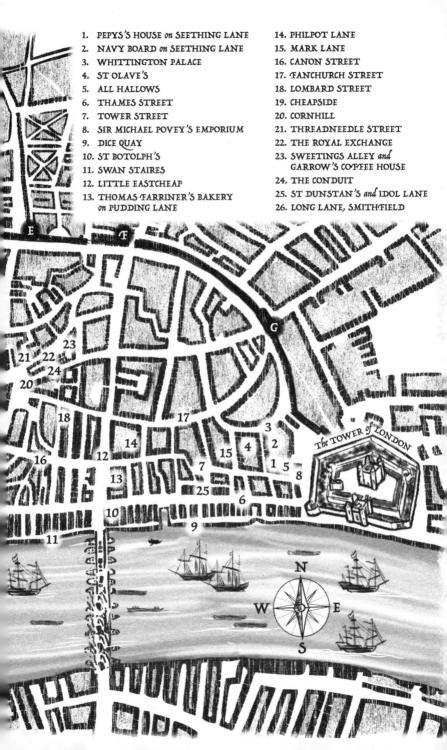

1. PEPYS'S HOUSE *on* SEETHING LANE
2. NAVY BOARD *on* SEETHING LANE
3. WHITTINGTON PALACE
4. ST OLAVE'S
5. ALL HALLOWS
6. THAMES STREET
7. TOWER STREET
8. SIR MICHAEL POVEY'S EMPORIUM
9. DICE QUAY
10. ST BOTOLPH'S
11. SWAN STAIRES
12. LITTLE EASTCHEAP
13. THOMAS FARRINER'S BAKERY
    on PUDDING LANE

14. PHILPOT LANE
15. MARK LANE
16. CANON STREET
17. FANCHURCH STREET
18. LOMBARD STREET
19. CHEAPSIDE
20. CORNHILL
21. THREADNEEDLE STREET
22. THE ROYAL EXCHANGE
23. SWEETINGS ALLEY *and*
    GARROW'S COFFEE HOUSE
24. THE CONDUIT
25. ST DUNSTAN'S *and* IDOL LANE
26. LONG LANE, SMITHFIELD

Chapter 1

Connor stared into the searing spotlights and felt his mouth go completely dry. A salty drop of sweat stung his right eye. He was transfixed, unable to move. His mind was completely blank.

His focus changed to the mass ranks of his school mates and their shuffling parents who stared back at him. Most of them were willing him to find the first words of a sentence. *Any sentence!* Others sniggered at the large, bewildered boy, dressed as the Pied Piper of Hamelin, surrounded by twenty embarrassed rats.

Connor opened his mouth again and the audience leaned forward, hoping to catch the first utterance from the star of the drama group's Christmas production. Ms DuFaye was whispering his opening line repeatedly at increasing volumes from the wings, until Connor remained the only person on stage or in the audience who didn't know what he was meant to say.

"Good citizens of Hamelin, I hear you have a problem," the director eventually called at full volume.

Connor couldn't actually hear *anything*, because his ears were blocked by a huge false beard. This was a last minute addition by Mrs Spencer to try to make him look older. She had stuck it on way too tightly. That, and the huge green hat which covered the bits the beard didn't, ensured Connor was deaf to any prompt.

In a complete panic, his thoughts darted around erratically, exactly when he needed to focus. Into his mind came the image of his best friend's magical map. Connor pictured it on Freddie's bedroom wall. If only it would appear in the school hall. *If only!* Connor would leap into the vortex to another time and place – *any* time and place but here, on this stage, right now.

Connor felt a sharp dig in his back. He turned to see the leading rat, Casey, mouthing at him. It sounded like, "Guusshh shizzizens uff Shammblin," Then the rat looked at the audience, raised her huge painted eyebrows and shook her head. Connor could definitely hear the wave of laughter that followed. This was all so unfair. He'd only joined the group in October because Ruby had signed up. She'd left after two weeks, citing 'artistic differences' with Ms DuFaye. *Great!* So he'd had to persevere. It would look suspicious if he went as well, wouldn't it? Everyone would rightly guess he fancied her.

What am I doing? Concentrate. Connor stared down at the recorder. He'd only started learning it five weeks ago... *'Play something!'* Connor lifted the instrument and with trembling breath he improvised a tune composed entirely of squeaks and squawks, to the amazement of the audience, rats and townspeople of Hamelin. Out of the corner of his eye he saw Ms DuFaye burying her head in her hands.

Connor's stage debut had got off to a disastrous start, but he suddenly picked out the encouraging faces of his friends Ruby and Freddie, smiling supportively and willing him on. Freddie's mum and dad were alongside, beaming positivity out of the semi-darkness.

Spurred on by their presence, his performance burst into life, until five minutes later when, much to everyone's amusement, and thanks to his nervous sweats loosening the grip of the glue, his beard fell off. It was highly embarrassing, but the bonus was he could suddenly hear and he only forgot his lines three more times during the first half.

Ms DuFaye's fiancé had composed a haunting tune with which the Piper would lure the rats away just before the interval, and then the children in the dramatic finale. Connor was making a good job of it second time round, but Casey, now playing the Mayor's child, accidentally on purpose trod on one of Connor's baggy trailing trouser legs. His humiliation was complete as they slowly started falling down, and as he confided to Freddie later, "You try playing the recorder, walking, remembering your lines, acting, and holding up your trousers at the same time."

He caught sight of Jasper, Kelvin and the gang on the front row, who had been made to attend as a detention. *They must be loving this*, Connor thought. The bully's sneering smile and menacing blue eyes tracked Connor's every move.

Jasper had been quiet since the episode at half term when Freddie, Connor and Ruby had left him and Kelvin encased in a frozen block of dirty washing and furniture, whilst they returned King Tutankhamun's precious scarab. But that would all change now. The final image of the Piper hopping off with his trousers round his ankles would be impossible to live down – ever!

Connor's completely disinterested mum and dad were the only people in a twenty-kilometre radius who had no idea about his disastrous acting debut.

Thankfully, Freddie's parents whisked Connor away from the crime scene for some 'celebration pizza'.

"You played a darlin' Piper, Connor. I thought you looked wonderful. A beard really suits you," gushed Freddie's mum.

"I can see why there were no rats left in Hamelin with *you* on the case, Connor. A career in pest control beckons!" Mr Malone added, less helpfully.

As Connor finished the pizza the others had no room for, he melted inside at their attempts to be kind, but he knew his debut had been a total disaster.

Freddie sported a fixed grin of support, and Ruby passed him half her garlic bread saying, "It's all right, I had some pasta with my brothers before the, er show." She gripped his hand and squeezed it twice during the meal. *That was definitely compensation for being bad in a play*, Connor thought later, rubbing the spot Ruby had touched and vowing never to wash it again.

It was now the Christmas holidays, which was a huge relief to all. Connor was glad to escape the teasing shouts of 'Pied Penguin' echoing down the school corridors, and Freddie was on antibiotics for a bad chest infection, which wouldn't clear up. And with school over for two weeks, Ruby had dyed the left side of her hair blue again, returning her to her preferred feisty look. Instead of meeting in the wintery cold at the old oak tree – their usual meeting place – Freddie and Connor headed over to Ruby's house, protected from any chance conflict with Jasper and his cronies. An added bonus of being at Ruby's was they could also avoid Finnegan and Kathleen, Freddie's very grumpy, deaf and elderly great uncle and aunt. They were staying until New Year whilst their new flat was decorated. Avoiding contact with Finnegan was best for all concerned, especially for Connor, who felt he was the unfair target of the old man's anger.

"Don't forget, RooBeeRoo," called Ruby's mum as she headed out to work. "Pick up the twins at four thirty. Text me when you've done it please. Their food's in the fridge."

Ruby cringed at her mum's use of her nickname in front of her friends, but Freddie hardly noticed; he seemed lost in his thoughts. "It's getting ready, I can feel it. We'd better be prepared, guys."

Next door, three packed rucksacks sat in Freddie's wardrobe, ready and waiting. Their contents were constantly refined and Connor's horde of sweets had been voted out, and more useful things put in its place, much to his dismay.

Whilst it had been Freddie's second adventure in the vortex, it had been Connor and Ruby's first, and they needed time to get their heads around what had happened last half term, when they were whisked 3,500 years back to Ancient Egypt. None of them knew when the magical world map would open again, and transport them along the vortex to a new destination.

After their Egyptian adventure, Freddie had started a replacement for his ruined notebook and had suggested the others do the same, so that now everyone had a copy if they got separated again. Four pages for each language, just as before, and now including Swedish, Japanese, Polish and with help from Mr Kapoor at the sweet shop, Hindi.

It was safe to be at Freddie's from 11 am until 3 pm, as his quarrelsome relations were out at various lunch clubs. That is, those that hadn't expelled Finnegan for his cantankerous behaviour. Life was certainly tricky in the Malone's house with him there.

"Family are family," Mr Malone pointed out, every time things got out of hand, until the day Finnegan drank most of a bottle of very special whiskey Mr Malone had been saving for Christmas. He wasn't so forgiving after that.

Freddie's bad winter cold had turned into a chest infection and he had been put on the strongest possible antibiotics and told to steer clear of Finnegan, who had only just recovered from a long illness himself.

Not a problem! Freddie thought.

Uncle Patrick had been absent for most of December. Freddie's favourite relation was badly missed. He lit up any room he entered. Laughter followed him, as if he sprinkled a magic dust that allowed everyone to see the best side of life. The rumour was he was going to stay throughout Christmas, and Freddie was already excited about what Patrick might bring. On his 13th birthday he'd given Freddie the enchanted map that hung on his bedroom wall. No present was ever going to top that. The colours were rich and luxuriant. Deep burgundy and reds, blues of all shades, and so many varieties of green he'd lost count. It was a living treasure. Orange deserts shimmered and sparkled. Flecks of quartz in the paint shot tiny shards of light into the room. All the major cities were illustrated with their landmarks: the Colosseum in Rome; the Kremlin in Moscow; and Niagara Falls still had a disconcerting habit of squirting water when he walked past. But they could all see the map was pulsing with energy and strength, and new symbols appeared hourly, teasing them with possibilities.

Recently, in addition to the god of the sea, Neptune, who blew wooden galleons about the Southern Oceans, the marbled figure of Atlas had appeared at the top of the map in the west.

Every hour, he would drop the huge globe from his shoulder and launch it, as if in a tenpin bowling alley. Freddie would shout "Strike!" as it collided with Stonehenge, before the stone circles were rebuilt immediately, and an angry druid shook his fist in Atlas's direction. The map was a great source of entertainment for Freddie.

In the Malone's house, Christmas excitement was mounting and the ritual of decorating their lounge and tree took place around the permanently seated elderly relations who criticised the placement of every light, bauble and piece of tinsel.

"Oh! Please hurry up, Patrick," Freddie heard his mother whisper as she hurried to make Kathleen her 100th cup of tea. Connor and Ruby had to be smuggled past the open lounge door into the cold night, both slipping down the icy path.

"Cinema at ten?" checked Freddie.

"Don't go anywhere without us," threatened Ruby playfully, clinging to the gatepost. Freddie watched Connor gingerly negotiate the pavement and slide away into the darkness.

Closing the door and turning back into the house, he found Finnegan blocking the hall. He spoke to Freddie at a fraction of his normal volume.

"Where are you off to, Freddie boy?"

"Nowhere. Err, she's just joking."

"Was that the girl with blue hair, and the fat boy?

You three are always very busy aren't you? Always up to something. What do—?" Just then a loud knock saved Freddie, and the welcome silhouette of Uncle Patrick showed through the frosted glass.

Freddie flung open the door and hugged his eccentric uncle as hard as he could. Then he stood back laughing because apart from carrying a huge bag of presents and a sack of clinking bottles, in the freezing December evening, Patrick was wearing shorts and a flashing Santa badge on his Hawaiian shirt.

Finnegan had vanished, but could still be heard. "The idiot with the silly shirts has arrived," he shouted to Kathleen. Uncle Patrick took a deep breath as he walked into the lounge, looking like a man entering a lion's cage.

After the evening meal, Freddie retreated to his room rather than watching TV with the volume loud enough to make your ears bleed – as Finnegan and Kathleen couldn't hear it otherwise. His mum came up a few minutes later with his antibiotics, and kissed him on the forehead. "I'm so sorry, darlin'. They're not here for much longer. Take your tablet now. I hope you're feeling better in the morning."

As soon as she closed the door, the world changed.

The lights flared with a fierce intensity like a lightning strike. Competing voices tumbled over each other, flying at Freddie from a thousand directions and meeting in the centre of his brain with perfect clarity. Swirling coloured beams played on the walls before swivelling and shooting to focus on the map. A rumbling wall of noise built behind it.

King Tutankhamun sneezed and the Yeti rushed over to wipe his nose. Suddenly everyone on the map looked ill. This felt so different from before. Freddie was mesmerised. Dramatic organ chords seemed to spell the end of the world. A feeling of doom clouded his mind.

Freddie pulled himself together and grabbed his rucksack. An electrical charge shot from the map to the door, and the sound of a hundred locks, bolts and chains, turned, clicked and rattled at once. Freddie crammed his tablets into his bag before texting:

SORRY – GOT TO GO

Neptune turned his head into the room and a chill wind made Freddie shudder even though he had his thick winter pyjamas on. He gasped as the sea god revealed the hidden side of his face which was covered in a bloody cloth. He blew the familiar tornado, causing Freddie's clothes and possessions to circle the room in a hectic dance. With his wide eyes fixed on the map, Freddie ran through a mental checklist of his backpack's contents, *Notebook, antibiotics, antiseptic, change of clothes – I'm ready for anything*, he said to himself. Suddenly, the map sprang to life as the cacophony grew. The colours of the different countries began changing, running back through history indicating their previous rulers.

Cloud formations slid across the continents like a weather report on fast-forward. The mighty oceans were alive and vast mountain ranges broke through the beautiful fabric.

Freddie watched as the Eiffel Tower shuddered, shrank and evaporated with a fizzle. His eyes were drawn upwards as the sea crashed against the White Cliffs of Dover. Then the Shard and Big Ben disappeared one after the other as the centuries scrolled back.

The River Thames surged from west to east across London, and a fraction of a second later a split followed its exact course, indicating the location of Freddie's next adventure.

Well at least I can speak the language! Freddie thought, trying to be brave.

All he could see now was his bedroom wall gaping wide open and the vortex appearing beyond. At the sound of all the locks, bolts and chains opening again, Freddie shot towards the wall, attracted by an invisible magnetic power. A thousand church bells sounded as ragged, bandaged hands beckoned him onwards and roughly pulled him through the gap.

Once again, he was on his way.

Chapter 2

Freddie's ears were still ringing as he hurtled headlong down the twisting vortex. Its purple and grey walls bounced him back into the jet stream, thrusting him faster and further on his journey. Portals rushed past on either side, like huge cinema screens. Each contained a possible destination, or in some cases, a reminder of a portal long closed and an adventure from the past. Nepal and Egypt sped by. The locations of his first two quests were now grey and static, closed off forever.

Hundreds of possibilities came and went as sirens, jet engines, opera singers and football chants exploded about Freddie. Letters, numbers and phrases swirled around, but at such speed he couldn't make out anything other than the words of the poem 'If—', the special homeward mantra which when recited would make the return portal appear and provide an escape route home. He hit his head on the wall and began to spin wildly, but kept hold of the rucksack, wishing desperately that Connor and Ruby were there to help. They had become such a brilliant team.

The Parisian portal flashed by on his left. Crowds were surrounding the guillotine and cheering another nobleman's execution. On his right, the First World War trench, previously mid battle, appeared quiet this time. In its place, was the breathtaking sight of a million poppies growing out of the drying mud.

Freddie suddenly panicked. *Oh no! I'm going to miss Christmas!* But if previous experiences were anything to go by, even if he was away for months on this adventure, it would only be a few hours back home. He really hoped the same rules would apply this time. Freddie's mouth watered at the thought of his mum's Christmas lunch and his dad's gravy. He couldn't miss that. *This had better be important,* he thought. He'd saved lives on both previous trips. Who knew what dangers lay ahead this time?

He came to rest by a portal through which he could see a huge cathedral. It was not one he recognised. He scanned the time code which was whirring as fast as ever at the bottom of the portal.

As Freddie watched, it turned from 1599 to 1600, but there was no feeling of urgency. He'd always been rushed before. This was different, as if he was early, or waiting for a bus. Then, with the clock spinning past 1650, the thick plasma surface rippled and softened, his signal to enter. But as Freddie was about to step through, he was grabbed roughly by the shoulders. He turned to see the familiar, terrifying cloaked figure, holding him back. As he tussled with the apparition, its bony grip slipped, allowing Freddie to pull away and burst through the portal, with just enough time to turn and see the retreating hooded phantom with the year set at 1665.

"Who *are* you?" Freddie hissed angrily. He'd been nothing but trouble in Egypt. At least he'd vanished now and not followed Freddie into his new reality.

Fresh sights, sounds and smells immediately assaulted his senses. It was warm compared to the winter he'd left, and just like a film set; full of costumes and cobbled streets.

Oh! No! Freddie had been transported to the 17th Century dressed in his Star Wars winter pyjamas. It was not a good look when you're trying to blend in.

He darted behind a line of twenty large wooden huts by the side of the cathedral. They all sold books. Ladies and gentlemen were promenading in their finery, surveying the leather-bound volumes, or dismissing a sales pitch from a stall owner.

Freddie delved into his rucksack and quickly chose his combat shorts and grey hoodie to change into. His eyes darted about, seeking as many clues as possible. A painted sign listed the service times of St Paul's Cathedral, but it wasn't the St Paul's he knew from his school trip to London two years ago. This was an ugly stone monster, with wooden scaffolding surrounding large sections that looked sturdier than the building itself.

It was the bustling street opposite that fascinated him. Horse-drawn carriages jostled pedestrians and burly tradesmen with handcarts skilfully skirted each other. Everyone seemed to be in a great hurry, all except the elegant book browsers, calmly bending to inspect volumes, causing their huge wigs to flop forwards at the side, like giant spaniel ears. Most men had mahogany canes with silver tops, and stockinged legs, knee-length breeches and embroidered frock coats under their giant hair-dos.

If the men looked fancy, then their wives and daughters were ten times so. Their garments were made from vibrant shiny fabrics that seemed to light up the drab streets around them, with huge skirts, hats and tight bodices in every colour. It looked like a fashion show. They all held fans, which constantly moved the stifling and very pungent air from under their noses. The other hand was hooked through the elbow of their partner, and occasionally dropped to lift their long dresses away from the animal dung that seemed to fill the cobbled streets.

It was a hectic scene. Dogs barked, children screamed and there were shouts of warning from speeding coachmen as the iron-shod wooden wheels clattered aggressively over the cobbles. Sweet smells and equally vile stenches filled Freddie's nose, so strongly he could almost taste them! After repacking his rucksack, he stood cautiously in the shadows observing and working out his next move. *Why have I been called here?* he wondered. *What's the emergency?*

He scanned the nearby row of shops. Customers flowed in and out of a baker's, a butcher's, two taverns, a dress shop, an apothecary and a cheese shop, which he could now smell above everything else. Freddie was beginning to relax. *What do I know about 1665? What's it famous for?*

As the mighty bells of St Paul's rang out high above him, several hands grabbed at his arms and tried to pull the rucksack from his back.

"Not you again!" said Freddie, turning to see not the shrouded figure as he had expected, but a dozen dishevelled urchins pawing at his clothes. They must have coordinated their attack with the bells to drown out some of the noise. Two or three of them held Freddie's arms, whilst the others worked on wrestling away his bag.

"Get off me!" shouted Freddie.

The ringleader was a stocky lad of about eight in a faded, but distinctive orange smock top. He had a mop of dark brown hair and a filthy face with piercing green eyes. "Speedy now. Be quick, you dogs! Should be easy pickings!"

Freddie struggled and by now several of the book browsers craned their necks to see what was happening. No one intervened, so he grabbed the rucksack as it was levered off his back and collapsed on top of it.

The gang tried to drag him off, but Freddie pulled their feet and tripped them up, sweeping his arms wildly about him. But now the kicks and punches were coming thick and fast.

Just as the assailants were getting the upper hand again, two elegant English accents cut through the fracas.

"Leave him alone, you vermin," said the first.

"Unhand this gentleman," boomed a second.

The urchins fled in all directions. Some scuttled down steps and through gaps in the stonework of the cathedral. As Freddie gathered up his bag, he was helped to his feet by the two young men.

"Thank you. You're very kind to help me. Thanks." He coughed and wiped blood from his mouth. The sun was setting behind his rescuers and Freddie had to shield his eyes against the bright light to make them out.

Before him stood two immaculately dressed, very dark-skinned slightly older boys, both a head or so taller than himself. They produced ornate patterned handkerchiefs and set about tending Freddie's wounds. As well as the blood trickling from his lip, his elbows were badly grazed.

"Ouch. Thanks," stuttered Freddie, as the taller boy in a blue frock coat dabbed at the corner of his mouth.

"It is my pleasure, sir. Allow me to introduce myself. I am Mingoe, indentured to Sir William Batten."

"And my name is Jack," said his red-coated friend with a huge smile that Freddie couldn't help but return, causing a yelp as his lip split afresh. "My employer is Sir William Penn. If you will allow, we will take you there where you can safely recover and change your clothes. These are torn beyond further use I'm afraid."

"No, I'm sure they'll... Ah! Yes, I see what you mean." His shorts and hoodie were ripped and filthy.

Mingoe shook his head. "Those dangerous ruffians are controlled by a vicious gang, and sent to pick on vulnerable targets." But then he continued more calmly, "May we enquire your name, sir?" As he did so, he bowed politely and revealed around his neck an engraved silver and brass collar that caught the light. "Your name, sir?" he asked again.

"Freddie Malone. But don't call me 'sir'. Just Freddie."

"But we have to," said Jack, his smile dimming for a second.

"You *have* to?" repeated Freddie, whilst Mingoe

attended his cuts.

"Yes, we are in the employment—"

"We're slaves," Mingoe cut in. His rescuers shared a look.

"Yes, we're slaves," Jack agreed, and for the first time his smile disappeared. Freddie was utterly speechless. He wanted to say a thousand things, but he felt stupid that he couldn't find the right words to express himself. He'd heard about slavery, but he hadn't been taught anything about it at school. He just knew it was wrong. How could you own another person? It was evil.

Mingoe and Jack guided him swiftly through the maze of packed, squalid streets, avoiding the open gutter in the centre that contained every vile substance known to man. The smell aside, he feasted on the sights and sounds walking to Seething Lane near the Tower of London.

Batten and Penn both declined to help Freddie, but they lived either side of Samuel Pepys esquire, an influential member of the Navy Board and close confidante and respected colleague of many fine lords. He even advised King Charles II and his brother James, the Duke of York. Pepys had been born in much humbler surroundings, but had raised himself up using his wits and education, to make himself indispensable to the British Navy. How did Freddie know all this? Because Pepys told him, in a speech that lasted nearly half an hour! He certainly wasn't shy.

Freddie was having trouble finding the reason he'd been called to 1665, but Pepys needed a servant and Freddie seemed to have magically appeared just at the right moment, so that was a good enough place to start.

Samuel's wife, Elizabeth, had tended to Freddie's cuts after Mingoe and Jack knocked on her door wondering if she could help. As soon as she heard Freddie's slight accent, she knew her husband would approve as he loved the people, music and literature of Ireland.

Freddie was dressed in brown blouse shirt and breeches, with beige stockings that matched his mousey brown hair. He was given black shoes with large silver buckles, and presented with a knock at the library door.

"If you can write neat and quick, and perform errands and household duties to my satisfaction, I'll see you pocket one pound a year, m'boy. No more, no less. That's the going rate. Take it or leave it!"

Pepys was a small, round-faced man, with an enormous dark-brown wig which tumbled over his shoulders. To test Freddie's secretarial suitability, he was dictating from scraps of paper brought home from his work at the Navy Board, hoping Freddie could fashion a presentable letter.

"Two hundred cannon on two first rate ships – two

hundred more between three second raters, and three thousand new recruited crew for the five ships, ready and able," Pepys continued in his surprisingly resonant voice.

A busy hour later, Pepys scanned the pages that Freddie had produced. Apart from two blotches where the quill split owing to excessive pressure, it looked excellent.

"Not at all bad, young Fred. You will serve m'purpose well. You'll learn fast, or find y'self back on the streets with the rascals that attacked you. What d'you say, boy?"

"Thank you, sir, I'm very happy to help here."

"Help! *Help!*" Pepys guffawed. "I think the word you're lookin' for is *serve*! You will *serve* here! Ha!" Pepys looked in a mirror and preened himself admiringly. "A servant is what you are, m'lad, and don't you ever forget it. Now rewrite that letter perfectly, without any blotches mind, and destroy my notes in the fire."

With that, Pepys strutted past his bookcases to the far end of his long library and picked up a violin. Freddie produced a perfect second attempt and sat back studying the notes Pepys had dictated from. He realised they were in shorthand, almost like a code. He then compared the notes and the letter until he began to see how it was formed. He hid the notes and first letter in his breeches whilst Pepys wasn't looking, and showed him the perfect second draft, which drew a satisfied intake of breath.

"Keep that up, m'boy, and you will find me a very happy master. M'wife will explain your other duties, now leave me to pleasure the neighbours with my musical scratchings." He laughed and dismissed 'Fred' with a wave of his violin bow.

Elizabeth was a pretty woman, although a little distracted, and distant. She seemed pleased that Freddie had passed the test and explained his night-time duties. "You're to make up the fires ready for the morning, and burn a fresh candle in the holder outside the front door to light people's way. Hang your master's clothes when he throws them off, and comb out his wig and set it on the block alongside the others. I'll tell you the morning duties after you've eaten something. Now be off with you." She smiled thinly at Freddie, and returned to her reading.

Later, as he lay in the tiny attic room with an inch of candle for light, he compared the coded notes with the final letter, and retrieving his battered rucksack from under the mattress, he listed all the major words he could translate. This was fun, seeing as there was no Wi-Fi or television to watch. The candle burned out and he lay pondering the wonders of the day. He wracked his brain trying to remember things about Pepys, but he'd remembered nothing except he kept some famous diaries. But surely he'd not been whisked to 1665 to be a good servant? *What's the real reason?*

After taking his antibiotics he drifted off to sleep on the lumpy mattress. *Are those fleas biting me?* he thought. *I hope not.*

Chapter 3

Freddie served Pepys his breakfast of beer, anchovies and pickled oysters. Then he forced down his own of tough bread and warm cheese, with 'small beer', a diluted version for children.

"It's unsafe to drink the water," Elizabeth warned him flatly. "You're not living by an Irish spring now! The Thames is a deathtrap."

Pepys had a busy morning ahead at the Navy Board and assigned Freddie his chores, alongside Mingoe and Jack, who would also be out on their masters' errands. There were some potions to pick up from an apothecary, provisions needed by the kitchen, and the posting of Pepys's correspondence to naval commanders at Portsmouth, Harwich and Plymouth.

England was in the midst of the second Anglo-Dutch War, which was mainly fought at sea, so the

Navy were incredibly important. From what Freddie could pick up, money was very tight and it was a real struggle for Pepys to keep the ships and men supplied with food, clothes and ammunition, let alone find funds to replace lost ships or repair damaged ones.

"You'll meet me at one o'clock by Ludgate. I have business in White Hall, and Westminster and I'll need you with me, young Fred", said Pepys as he strode off along Seething Lane to the Navy Board. He called over his shoulder, "Mingoe and Jack will instruct you on procedures. And may God guard you against the pestilence. At any rate, don't bring it home to me. Look lively now."

Freddie stopped in his tracks. "Pestilence!" he said, "What pestilence?" Mingoe and Jack were by his side.

"You haven't heard? The plague has returned, and the numbers are growing," Mingoe told him.

"Most years we have plague deaths," Jack added calmly. "Haven't you had it in Ireland?"

"Yes... err, yes of course. The plague. Wow!"

"Wow?" said Mingoe. "What does that mean?"

"It means, I hope we don't catch it," said Freddie quickly.

"Watch what we do and you'll be safe," said Jack. "And don't touch animals or strangers," he added emphatically as they set off through the cramped, noisy streets. At times passageways were so packed it was impossible not to brush past people. Children constantly pulled at arms or wrists, asking for money. But Mingoe and Jack cut a magnificent swathe through the throng. They looked amazing in their fine costumes, and their skin colour stood out amongst the crowds of curious pale faces. They were tall, strong and proud and Freddie felt very protected by his new friends.

All three had duties at the General Letter Office on Threadneedle Street, the forerunner of the Post Office, Freddie supposed. Here, the clerk, or window man as he was known, took Freddie's large bundle of letters with a heavy sigh.

"Tell your master to settle his debts. I'll not take any more from him after today, unless he pays what's outstanding."

"Yes, sir, I'll tell my—"

But the gruff and sweaty man swished him away. Freddie turned and caught a glimpse of a shrouded figure dart behind a passing carriage. It sent a shiver down his spine. *Please don't let him be here*, he thought.

"What's the matter?" asked Mingoe gently.

"I just thought… I was just worried about the plague," Freddie fibbed. But he *was* worried: about the figure, *and* the plague. He hoped whatever had called him to 1665 would send him back in one piece. Luckily, he was still taking his antibiotics. *Hopefully they'll help*, he thought to himself as they moved off along Cheapside.

This was the widest and busiest street in the city, packed with shops and coffee houses, carriages and sedan chairs. Everyone seemed to be going about life as normal. They soon reached Ludgate where Freddie parted with his new friends and waited for Pepys.

The City of London was surrounded by a huge wall at least six metres high. Mingoe explained that there were seven gates in the wall, of which Ludgate was one, through which every*one* and every*thing* came into the city. The congestion was considerable. It seemed that the louder you shouted and the faster you approached, the quicker you got through. *Jasper would do well here*, Freddie thought.

Just after one o'clock, a flustered Pepys appeared. He beckoned Freddie into a carriage, and away they raced to White Hall, about three kilometres outside the city walls.

Freddie was fascinated watching London pass by as they trotted down Fleet Street. He'd walked this route with his mum and dad, and it was weird not to see Nelson on his column as they turned from the Strand into King's Street. But of course, it wouldn't be built for nearly two hundred years.

"Sir, the 'window man' said he will not send any more of your letters until the bill is paid."

Pepys looked cross. "Curse the lot of 'em. Can they not see the work I'm doing? I need ten pairs of hands to complete the jobs I undertake."

The carriage stopped outside the grand fortified gatehouse of the Palace of White Hall, and Pepys enquired, "Where's the king?" He was pointed in the direction of St James's Park, and the carriage sped into very formal and well-laid-out gardens with grassland beyond.

They approached a group of dazzlingly dressed men and women by a large lake. About 40 people were feeding swans and pelicans that gorged on the delicacies offered them. The animals appeared much better fed than the majority of people Freddie had just passed in the streets. A herd of antelope grazed contentedly as Pepys and Freddie climbed down from the carriage and approached on foot.

Pepys pointed at the tallest man. "Be silent and attentive. Don't show me up in any way. Bow and scrape the ground when I do. Is this the first time you've met a king?" Pepys didn't even wait for Freddie to respond, so sure was he that this Irish youth would never have been in the presence of royalty. Now was not the time for Freddie to tell Pepys he had spent months as King Tutankhamun's closest friend!

Pepys continued, "Look, there's the royal crane."

"The what?" Freddie asked politely, unsure he'd heard properly.

"The bird. The crane King Charles is feeding – it has a wooden leg. One of my shipbuilders crafted a peg for the bird that lost its original in a squabble. The king dotes on it." He turned to Freddie. "Two paces behind me, boy. You're not my son, you're my servant."

Freddie dropped back as they neared the cluster of courtiers, where all but five discreetly left, as the king and the Duke of York greeted Pepys.

King Charles II had an enormous brown wig that finished nearly thirty centimetres below his shoulders. He had a weedy moustache and long nose, but kind eyes and a ready smile. His brother James had a dark-blonde wig and a thinner face, but with the same distinctive nose and a calm demeanour. His advisors gathered in a semi-circle behind, anxious for Pepys's news.

"Your Majesty." Pepys bowed so low he almost licked the grass. Freddie did likewise. "Your Royal Highness, my lords. I bring some good news from the Navy Board. I have, with great difficulty, made provision to supply the noble Duke of York with new ships and men for the action he hopes to undertake against the Dutch. It has taken many weeks of hard work on my behalf to ensure the Navy has the best…"

"Yes, Pepys, we know how hard you work, you tell us so often," said Charles playfully.

"Yes, Your Majesty. I only mention it, as it becomes harder and harder to find the funds to supply the ships which will win us the war. I would humbly beg your good council and our parliament to release more so we can bring a speedy end to this hateful conflict." Freddie noticed several of the men behind the king aim disdainful looks at Pepys.

"Indeed, you speak wisely. If I am to send my dear brother off to fight, I must ensure he has the means to do so. I will demand more resources for my Navy, but spend it wisely, Pepys. The men behind me will want to know the cost of each square inch of sail and ship's biscuit."

"Yes, Your Majesty."

James, Duke of York, smiling for the first time, enquired, "What new provision is made?"

Pepys, flustered by the dark looks he was receiving, referred to a clutch of papers he held and sifted through, unable to find the details he needed.

"They are somewhere, Your Majesty..."

The semi-circle of advisors tilted their heads and smirked, enjoying Pepys's discomfort. Neither the king nor the Duke of York enjoyed being kept waiting and their raised eyebrows and direct gaze made him even more uncomfortable.

"I'm sorry, Your Majesty, I can't..." Pepys was consumed with embarrassment. "I can't..."

"Two hundred cannon on two first rate ships. Two hundred more between three second raters, and three thousand new recruited crew for the five ships, ready and able," intervened Freddie calmly and quietly from behind Pepys's shoulder. Pepys produced a shy smile and repeated, "Yes, Your Highness, all ready and able."

The king's eyes flicked to the slight, mousey haired boy and he smiled generously. "Bravo, young man!

46

Your name?"

"Freddie Malone, Your Majesty."

"An Irishman, brother James, what do you make of that?"

"Well he has memory and nerve, that's for sure. Like most Irishmen!" Everyone laughed, even eventually Pepys.

Not wanting to upset his master, Freddie retreated into his shadow, and studied the fine ladies who were spoiling six overweight yapping King Charles Spaniels. Freddie couldn't believe the situation he found himself in, and tried to remember everything.

As the audience came to an end, he and Pepys bowed again. They walked backwards, so as not to turn their backs on the king, unable to see quite where they were treading. The king said, "Mr Malone, look after your master, he is very precious to us."

"Yes, Your Majesty. As you are to him." The king clapped his hands twice in polite recognition of the compliment and the royal party returned to the ladies feeding the pelicans.

"Well, that all went very well I think," said Pepys as they walked to the carriage.

"Yes, sir," said Freddie, who was more concerned that at this point in history poop-a-scooping hadn't been invented, and began to thoroughly clean both pairs of shoes on the grass. Then Pepys turned to him and gave him a silver penny. "Keep it up, boy. Keep your eyes 'n' ears open and remember who feeds and clothes you. These are turbulent times and a man must be sure of his friends."

It must be his way of saying thank you, thought Freddie, as they set off for Westminster where Pepys had business.

Around the parliament buildings, important people held meetings and exchanged updates about the war, the economy and the plague. Pepys disappeared, shouting back to Freddie, "Wait for me by Cromwell's head." Freddie thought that must be a pub, but he couldn't see a sign. He asked a soldier who was guarding a gateway. He simply pointed up to the south end of Westminster Hall, where on top of a pole was the unmistakable sight of a head. Cromwell's head! It was Oliver Cromwell's *actual* head! Complete with hair, taut, wind-blown skin, and only his eyes missing – it was a gruesome sight to behold. Freddie couldn't stop looking at it.

"That's what 'appens. One day you're top of the pile, and the next you're atop a spike, with no-*body* to keep you company." The soldier chuckled, but Freddie couldn't bring himself to laugh at the joke. He shuddered.

Passing through Covent Garden on the journey back, the coach stopped. Pepys rattled his cane on the wooden side and asked the driver, "What's the hold-up?" But there was no answer. They scrambled out and peered up at the man holding the horses' reins, who was sitting still and breathing heavily, obviously very sick. Pepys gave Freddie sixpence. "Leave that on the seat next to him, but don't touch anything else mind." Freddie did as instructed, with his heart pounding, as two ladies from a flower stall came to help the man.

"S'all right, love, we'll look after 'im. He lives up by St Giles. We'll send fer 'is wife."

Pepys left them to deal with the man, who was sweating badly and talking nonsense. He had a haunted look in his eyes. Freddie thought he'd seen his first plague victim.

On foot, they cut down Drury Lane, which was eerily deserted. The reason soon became obvious. They came upon a door with a red cross painted on it, and the words, 'The Lord have mercy on this house'. Pepys backed away as if he'd seen a ghost, and Freddie only just stopped him from reversing into another door opposite with the same daubed slogan. Freddie felt like every breath they took was a risk. He was desperate to get away.

Pepys whispered urgently, "Never did I think I'd see it. I hoped I never would. This is a disaster in the heart of London! We must leave now, quickly." Freddie nodded, all his senses screaming panic. They increased their speed, and as they passed a third house with the same woeful plea painted on its door, they saw a young

49

woman at the window holding a child, gently bouncing it in her arms, trying to pacify its cries. Her eyes pleaded with Freddie and he desperately thought of how he could help. He ran to the window and placed his silver penny on the sill. A temporary smile lit the face of the young mother. Freddie retreated and she opened the window just enough to retrieve the coin. As she did so, Freddie could see huge purple marks on her inner forearm and felt a wave of sympathy for the young woman.

Pepys hissed at him impatiently, "Quickly, boy! Are you trying to kill us both? It's very sad of course, but to save others we must save ourselves. Don't put yourself in danger, or you will bring the pestilence upon me. Promise me. Swear on it, boy!"

Freddie stammered, "I swear, sir," but all he could think of was the face of the woman and the fate that awaited her and her baby.

Pepys pressed another silver penny in Freddie's hand. "I saw what you did... You are a kind and clever lad. But remember, kind and clever don't always win the day. Mix it with steel and strength. That's when kind becomes powerful."

"Yes, sir," said Freddie, slowly warming to his master.

Chapter 4

Ruby called for Freddie, but Uncle Patrick opened the door, "He's back at the doctor's getting some more tablets. The little scamp lost the last lot. I'll tell him you knocked. Where will you be?"

"The cinema. Our usual place. Thank you."

"Who's that?" Finnegan shouted from inside. "Is that the *Amazonians* delivering my hot water bottle?"

"I've got to go, Ruby. I'm *baby*-sitting," Uncle Patrick said, and they shared a knowing smile.

Ten minutes later Ruby was safely hidden with Connor behind the huge cardboard cut-out figures from next week's blockbuster on the mezzanine level of the cinema. This was the perfect winter hideaway with great views out over the High Street and atrium, through the floor-to-ceiling glass.

Approaching enemies were easily spotted, and it was certainly warmer than sitting up in the oak tree, their normal meeting place.

"When did you get the text?" asked Ruby.

"This morning when I woke up."

"Same here. I tried calling him, but no answer."

It was only 10:30 am, but Connor had already finished his packed lunch. He reluctantly accepted some lentil crisps Ruby offered, and only warmed to them after the third handful. They were both annoyed to have missed out on the adventure, but excited to hear what Freddie had to tell them. Eventually a message pinged through to their group chat:

FINISHED AT DOC'S. ON MY WAY

Freddie arrived, cleaning his hands with a wet-wipe and sporting a smile that gave away his news.

"No! We've missed it, haven't we?" Ruby cried. "I said don't go anywhere without us. Aarrgghh! Tell us where you've been."

"I jusss ssknew it," said Connor, now through a mouthful of popcorn.

"London," Freddie said calmly, wiping between his fingers.

"London?" they repeated in sync.

"Yep! London." Freddie smiled at them and waited. He was enjoying this.

"So, you've been to Nepal, Egypt and now...

London." Ruby laid out the statement like a lawyer in court.

Freddie nodded. "Yep."

"Well, we've all been to London before," said Connor, beginning to feel like he hadn't missed out too badly.

"Ah! But when?"

"Oh! Right I see what you..." Ruby twigged. "Well *tell* us, then."

"1665!"

"1665? Wow!" said Connor.

"1665? I can't believe it." Ruby was so excited. "Tell us. Come on!" She had been puzzled by his unusually thorough hand-cleansing routine, but suddenly jolted back as if pulled by a string. She whispered, "1665. London. Great Plague! Wow, buddy, you'd better spill the beans."

"Plague?" spluttered Connor. "What plague?"

An hour later they were up to date with King Charles II, Pepys, Mingoe, Jack and the plague houses on Drury Lane. Ruby smiled.

"Amazing! You legend, Freddie. I can't believe it."

"What happened next?" urged Connor.

Freddie took a swig from his drink bottle, gulped and shook his head. "Clean water! I'll never take it for granted ever again." He sat back against the huge glass window and continued.

"We all lived in a line on Seething Lane, in these big houses, near the Tower of London. Mingoe on one side, and Jack on the other. They showed me the ropes and we all did our jobs and errands together.

"As the days went on, I saw the plague take hold, and I realised I must have been called there because of it. So I tried to find out as much as I could.

"New laws had been passed trying to stop the disease spreading. Whenever a house had a victim inside, the whole family had to be locked up with them for forty days and not allowed out in case they carried it. In the early weeks a 'watchman' with a spear was put outside the front door to make sure no one went in or out. But the trouble was a lot of them were easily bribed, and people were allowed to leave who shouldn't have been, spreading the sickness further and faster.

"Plus, there were these old ladies called 'searchers of the dead', who charged fourpence to go into a house and examine the body. It was up to them to say how that person had died. But loads of *them* were corrupt as well, and people gave them jewellery and money to lie. The searcher would then say the person had died from something else and not the plague. It was ridiculous. If people hadn't been so dodgy and greedy, it wouldn't have spread like it did.

"Then gangs took over, controlling the watchmen and the searchers and they got very rich, very quickly. The most vicious was a gang called the Packers.

"We sat by St Paul's one day and Mingoe pointed out the ringleaders who operated the gang from the cathedral crypt. The Packers also had a huge warehouse down by the Thames on Dice Quay. They controlled dozens of villains who did their dirty work.

"We went into the cathedral and it was really wrecked and filthy.

"There had been this massive civil war years before I arrived and Mingoe told me that 800 soldiers and horses had lived in there. There were stalls selling fruit and fish, and animals wandering about. There was even a game of nine-pins going on, like ten pin bowling, but with people betting on it. It wasn't like a church at all. It was a real tip.

"Outside it was easy to spot the gang of kids as they came up the steps from the crypt, just before the bell rang on the hour. This boy with the orange top—"

"The one that attacked you?" asked Connor like a TV detective.

"Yeah. Him. He was a right little thug, and he

got told who to attack by a huge man who stood on the scaffolding and sent signals. Mingoe, Jack and I went and stood near their target, pretending to talk to each other, just enough to put them off. Then Mingoe would tell the person how lucky they'd been, and warn them about being alone in this part of the city.

"We only managed it for a couple of afternoons as the thugs began watching us, and Mingoe and Jack really stood out because of their skin colour and posh bright coats. But we'd saved six people from being robbed by then.

"I didn't think that was why I'd been called to 1665 though. As we walked away, I looked back and saw an old woman sitting up on the scaffolding, smoking a pipe. She was just staring at us. Next to her sat a toothless girl playing with a long knife, and then the huge man who gave the signals. All three of them had their eyes fixed on us. We got out of there pronto."

"Why don't the Watch do something about them?" Freddie asked.

"The Watch are of no use. You're better off calling for unicorns," said Jack. "Once, we were surrounded by an angry mob who didn't like us because of our skin. To them, it was as if we were responsible for everything bad in their lives. People were angry because food was scarce, work was badly paid, and they were being poisoned by foul water. All at once they turned on us, as if it was our fault." Jack fell silent, and Mingoe took up the tale.

"We called for the Watch to help us, but they were scared. A few decent people tried to make the mob see sense, but they wouldn't listen to reason."

Jack continued, "They closed in on us and were spitting and throwing things, there was madness in their eyes. I realised we only had a few seconds to save ourselves. Then, from deep inside, I remembered my father and uncles chanting the 'Dance of the Dead'. It was so powerful, so strong. I just started to copy it, there and then. I filled my lungs and chanted words I was half making up and half remembering."

"It sounded like a powerful lost language, a spell," Mingoe told Freddie, "and I could see it was working. The mob stopped and went quiet, unsure of what to do. I joined in and I turned it into a war dance. I was so angry that they were treating us like this, but I soon realised *we* were frightening *them* with our jumps and chants. I decided to make it look like I was putting spells on them, and as soon as I did that, they turned and ran away."

"I copied Mingoe," said Jack, "and now we were advancing on them. They scattered, screaming that we were devils. Then *my* Sir William arrived in a coach and rescued us. He'd been alerted and he took us away, laughing off what had happened."

"Our 'Dance of the Dead' had saved our lives. But we wondered afterwards that it might only confirm to those stupid people that we *were* devils, and they would build up more anger towards us. But Sir William said that they weren't clever enough to think like that. They were a mob, and a mob just follows the loudest voice at the time. Tomorrow they will follow the next shouting man."

Freddie wished he could think of something to say that would comfort his friends, but as so often happened, words just weren't enough. He said, "I'm so sorry you had to go through that." But that sounded so completely lame in relation to what they'd endured.

Later that night, Pepys was having difficulty finding a carriage after attending a meeting of the Royal Society. This was a very important organisation full of the most brilliant scientists and philosophers, writers and engineers. "The most progressive minds of the day," Pepys had said enthusiastically on the way there. He delighted in watching the experiments on dead animals and people. Machines were demonstrated, theories argued, solutions were sought and travel tales were shared. Freddie sneaked in at the back, and hid with only his eyes above the barrier of the tiered lecture theatre at Gresham College.

It had been his job to secure a carriage for the

return to Seething Lane, but by the time he had dragged himself away from a lecture about 'The Flea' from Robert Hooke, all the transport was taken. Pepys had to engage a 'lanthorn' boy to light their journey through the dark streets.

The boy was small, and would easily pass for a six-year-old, though Freddie guessed he was probably nine. He was like a pixie, with lively, quick jerky limbs, and thick ginger hair on top of a grimy face and a mischievous smile.

"What's your name?" Freddie asked him.

"Billy Jenks," he replied in a husky voice and wiped his nose on his sleeve. "Me an' Ma live in Alsatia." Which, Freddie learned, was a terrible slum south of Fleet Street, full of lawless cutpurses and villains. With his hand on his sword, Pepys scuttled along behind out of earshot, as Billy boasted, "I know London like no other. I know every alley, dock and hideaway. That's why I've not been taken."

"Taken?"

"Yeah! Boys like me disappear. Either a gang nabs you and teaches you to rob, or the Navy takes you to sweat on a ship, or the traders thieve you to sail to the Indies and work the plantations. And it's not just boys. Women, and girls get snatched as well. They're taken to the New World, so Ma says. People set traps to catch children, pretend to be kind, and then sell 'em. You can't trust no one, I tell you. My dad..." Billy fell silent. His confidence evaporated.

"Your dad what?" asked Freddie.

"My dad's missing," Billy admitted in a small voice. "It's just me and Ma now. She says he's been snatched. 'Appens all the time. She says fifteen hundred were taken in a single week once... taken to fight on the ships. How many's fifteen hundred?"

"A lot," said Freddie.

"I can count to thirty. Well, nearly thirty. Is it more than that?"

"Yes. It's much more than thirty," said Freddie.

"I don't know numbers, but I know how to hide all right. I take the coins I earn back to Ma, and she feeds the family what took us in. And all night I light people's way home. And all the time I look for my dad, in the alleys and doorways. I'm gonna find him one day, I know it. I'm gonna find him in the shadows."

"I hope so, Billy. But where can I find *you* again?"

"Why? You're not with the press gang are you?" Billy's face darkened with mistrust.

"No, I'm not. I just might need help sometime, and I can't think of anyone better than you."

"You're a wise judge an' all, mate. Always by the 'free-etters' at curtain down.

"Do you mean theatres?"

"Yeah! Free-*Etters*. After that, by the taverns on Cheapside to light home the last wobblers." He imitated drunken walking, and Pepys called out, "Steady there,

60

boy, light my feet, not the walls. That's not what you've been paid for." Billy laughed and showed Freddie the paltry farthing in his hand that Pepys had given him before setting off, and wiped his continually runny nose for the twentieth time.

"Always get paid up front or don't set off, that's my advice."

They arrived in Seething Lane, and as Billy doused his flaming reed torch in the horse trough outside Pepys's house, for the second time that day Freddie gave away a silver penny, and made a friend for life.

Chapter 5

Every half an hour people poured out from the separate cinema screens and passed by the hidden trio. Freddie would pause for a moment, sanitise his hands again, and then carry on sometimes closing his eyes as he struggled to remember details.

"I just couldn't get clean. Everything was dirty. The Tower of London was already six hundred years old when I was there, and it was filthy, it was almost black. I liked it best when we were on the river. The Thames was like a motorway through the city, with hundreds of boats called 'wherries' ferrying people about, and big barges full of cargo. It was so much easier travelling on the water than through the crazy streets.

"I went with Pepys up river from Tower Wharf to London Bridge, and on to Westminster. It was fantastic. For a start, all along the shoreline in front of these huge warehouses were separate quays with boats loading and unloading. Then there were these upright metal cages on poles that stuck out of the water. They had the skeletons of pirates inside.

"Pepys told me, 'Pirates are covered in pitch and set in a cage - a lesson for anyone else who thinks it's a good idea... after thirty years or so, their bones fall apart and drop in the water.'

"How many were there?" asked Connor, fascinated.

"Loads and loads. I saw about twenty." Freddie grimaced, shuddering at the memory. The bridge was amazing though. It was the only way to cross the Thames so it was always packed. There were houses and shops along most of it, except the northern end near the city where they'd all burned down years before.

"Pepys said, 'There's an old saying Fred, *the bridge was built for wise men to go over, and fools to go under*, which is not far from the truth. At certain times the tide gushes between the legs the bridge stands on. It becomes lethal. Many have drowned.'

"He was always pointing things out to me and telling me interesting stuff. It was great! There were nineteen arches under the bridge. I counted them!"

"Saddo!" Ruby smiled.

"Yeah I know. But only four of them were

safe to row through. There were even traffic jams there. All sorts of things floated past in the water. Wooden crates, rubbish, dead animals. It was rank. I wouldn't have wanted to fall in, but at least you got a breeze in the boat, and it wasn't quite as stinky as the alleys.

"On one street I watched a woman pour a bucket of something horrible out of a top-floor window, down into the road. She called, 'Watch out below', but didn't actually give people time to get out of the way. They all shouted up at her and a big argument started, so she poured another lot out!

"All the time, smoke made your eyes water, your nose run, and it scratched your throat. People just burned anything on their fires. I had a cough for weeks."

"Weeks?" asked Connor. "How long were you there?"

"Hang on, I'll tell you, just let me tell it in order so I don't forget stuff."

"Yeah, zip it, Conman!" Ruby playfully poked Connor in the ribs.

"Most days, after our jobs, Mingoe and Jack showed me around. We used to sit near a shop in Cheapside market where the smells of freshly baked bread mixed with fantastic spices masked the stench of the nasty stuff. You could get fresh water at the Standard on Cornhill, and nearby there was Garraway's coffee house where fancy gentlemen just sat talking and reading news sheets and pamphlets. They were all really excited about tea and hot chocolate which were the latest fashion and really expensive.

"Then one night in early June, I met this amazing chemist guy. He was an apothecary called William Boghurst, and Pepys asked him to give a talk in his library to sixty or so important friends, because the plague was getting nearer the city walls. I was serving food and drinks, but I heard nearly all of it."

Boghurst was young, about thirty or so Freddie thought, and really thin. He was the leading authority on the plague. What he had to say was frightening and fascinating. Freddie listened as best he could, while trying to serve his master's important guests.

"Gentlemen, London faces its sternest battle. Hundreds have died already and without question thousands more will. Let me explain how our enemy appears.

"Imagine your wife or daughter, if you will. She may wake with a cold on a Friday morning. By lunch, which she refuses, it has progressed from a mild to a burning fever, and her blood is already poisoned. Then headaches follow which turn severe, with dizziness and convulsions. By Friday evening her eyesight dims, the sockets red and sore from scratching. Overnight, strange buboes and pustules grow in the groin and armpit. These are full of puss that either burst outwards or discharge into her blood system.

"Rosettes, or 'Pestilential tokens' adorn her skin. Black or purple, they signal a rapid decline. She sleeps little, but tosses and turns, sweats and swears, until as light comes on Saturday she can take no loud noise. Then, soon after, deafness strikes. She has vile breath, hoarseness of voice, her throat is full of razors, her mouth dry, with an unquenchable thirst.

"Sometime in the afternoon the nauseous sickness begins, with retching, vomiting and loose bowels, and a second night of torturous pain.

"Sunday brings terrible side stitches, back spasms, constant sweats, spots, blains and blotches all over the skin. The Sabbath, instead of comfort, brings carbuncles, weak pulse and faintness of heart. Paranoia is followed by absolute madness, and, as a blessed mercy before the day is out, a searing screaming death ends her mortal journey. And so one more number is added to the tally of the lost."

There was absolute silence in the room. No one moved. The young man continued, "And this, gentlemen, is to describe but half of the suffering our fellow citizens are enduring. As if their lives have not been hard enough. It is rapidly becoming a disease of the poor, as all us men of means and substance can afford to leave London for our country houses to avoid the contact. But, the very people who *should* stay – the doctors, the physicians, the apothecaries, the educated and the organised – these people are the first to flee, saving themselves and not their fellow man. An ungodly act, in my opinion."

Freddie looked around the room at the rows of bewigged, finely dressed, powerful and influential men, and wondered, *Who would stay and help, who would run to save themselves?* It was a very difficult question.

A fierce knocking on Pepys's door had Freddie racing from the room to answer. It was a breathless messenger from the Navy Board. Freddie showed him into the Library. Boghurst stepped aside as the excited man immediately addressed the assembled group. "A great victory, my lords. For this day our noble Duke of York has, at a mighty sea battle near Lowestoft, defeated the Dutch in glorious manner. Let London rejoice. Let England salute the news, and thank God for King Charles and his noble brother James."

There was an outburst of joy in the room. Whereas a minute before they'd been thunderstruck, reliving the final moments of a plague victim, now they were back slapping, cheering and toasting. Only Freddie saw the messenger hand Pepys a separate message. Pepys opened a bookcase and slid it unread between two of his many books. And only Freddie saw Boghurst collect his papers and walk calmly around the side of the room and down the stairs into the jubilant street scene outside. He walked well away from the crowds, hugging the shadows.

As Freddie watched on, he saw another dark shape move fifty metres or so away and disappear into the night. *Was that the shrouded man?* Freddie strained his eyes to see, but was ordered inside by Pepys.

"Bring wine, sac, beer and malmsey. Bring it all. We have a great deal to celebrate," cried his master.

Freddie carried large quantities of Pepys's precious wine collection upstairs to the rowdy gathering that night.

As the hours passed, Pepys's wig slipped to an alarming angle. He and his friends got wilder and less comprehensible. Freddie was amazed and thought the world was going mad. Had they already forgotten Boghurst and his predictions?

And, why was the shrouded man lurking, if it was him? In Egypt he had definitely wanted the scarab and elixir, so what was he after in London? Freddie's mind whirled. But he guessed he'd soon find out.

Morning saw Elizabeth in a foul mood, ordering servants around in a loud voice from just outside the dining room where Pepys was sleeping.

"She's doing it on purpose," laughed Cook, a mighty woman with strong opinions. "She's paying him back for last night. I don't blame her."

A few minutes later a bedraggled Pepys emerged

with his clothes askew and his wig perched on top of his flattened night hat, which made everyone secretly smirk. He began shouting even louder than his wife and everyone scattered.

Freddie looked at Ruby and Connor with a little glint in his eye. "It was then that I remembered the hidden message in the bookcase. So I slipped into the library and grabbed it. *Great!* Except it was in Latin. But it was written in a beautiful turquoise ink.

"I heard Pepys coming so I hid it again, but on a different shelf, so I could find it later. And he was so wobbly I doubt he even remembered getting it!"

Ruby and Connor laughed, but then Ruby grabbed Connor's arm.

"Jasper and Casey just walked in," she whispered.

Connor felt physically sick at the sight of Jasper, who strutted arm in arm with the heavily painted Casey. She had been promoted to gang-leader's sidekick, displacing the sulking hanger-on, Kelvin, who trailed behind. Ruby whispered, "Her eyebrows aren't real, they look like two dancing slugs."

When the coast was clear, the three friends slipped unseen into the cold afternoon.

"I'll carry on tomorrow," said Freddie, leaving Connor outside the fish and chip shop.

"Same again, ten at the cinema?" asked Ruby.

"Yeah, good for me."

Connor nodded. "And me."

Leaving him to get in the queue, Freddie and Ruby wandered off through the Christmas streets towards their end of town, waving as they went.

Connor looked down at his knuckles where he'd touched Freddie a moment before, remembering how often his best friend had cleaned his hands during the day. He asked politely for a hand wipe with his sausage, cod and chips.

Best to be safe, he thought.

Chapter 6

"So, buddy, last night, did you fly off anywhere without us?" Ruby grinned and nudged Freddie as they rushed through the automatic doors into the warm cinema foyer. "I'm not letting you out of my sight. I want to go to London and help those guys. What did the Latin letter say?"

Freddie smiled back. "That bit's coming up..." Freddie stopped as they reached the windows. "Hey, that's weird. Where's Connor? He's usually first. I'll text him."

"I tried an hour ago. No reply," said Ruby.

"I'll call," said Freddie. "Voicemail! Hello, mate. 'RooBeeRoo' and—"

"Shut up!" laughed Ruby, cringing as Freddie used her mum's nickname for her.

"We're waiting. Are you buying our Christmas

pressies? Ruby's mad at you because she wants to hear what happened next."

She grabbed the phone. "Shut up! I'm not mad at you, Conman, just move yourself."

So they waited... and waited...

Connor had every reason to be late. As he cut through the mall car park he saw Jasper's gang clustered around an old man in a big hat. It was very early for the gang to be out and about. They were all nodding but Connor had no idea what was being said, because the little old man, was facing away.

Connor hid behind the row of recycling bins and watched on. He saw the old man hand an envelope to Jasper, who stuffed it in the back pocket of his joggers. *What's going on? Why was Jasper taking something from an old guy?* Connor was just about to make an escape when Casey and two other rats from the Christmas show walked round the corner and stopped right in front of him.

"What you doing hiding by the bins?" Casey said, then called to Jasper, "Hey, 'J-J', look who's been digging in the bins looking for his breakfast?" Her companions giggled, but Connor's stomach turned to concrete.

Jasper and his track-suited gang swaggered over with great relish. Connor tried to leave, but was barred by the three girls. He just caught sight of the old man's back disappearing around a corner.

"Well, well, it's the Pied Penguin! Looking for scraps are you? Not fat enough?" With his arm around Casey, Jasper fizzed with strength and danger. Connor prepared himself for a barrage of abuse, but it was Casey who started.

"You're pathetic! You made us all look stupid. You can't act and you can't play music. You should just crawl into a hole and stay there," she snarled. Her eyebrows were even bigger and a different shape to yesterday. Connor stood with his head bowed, praying for it to end. He caught a glimpse of the envelope in Jasper's back pocket.

The bully's eyes flashed. "No Case, you've got it wrong. This is Fatboy Massey. He's on a world tour. Didn't you see him on breakfast telly? And guess what? He's come to play a concert here!"

"What?" piped up Kelvin.

"Shut up, Kel! Fatboy's going to entertain the Christmas shoppers." Connor felt a bolt of terror strike through him. He cast a frantic look around for help, but he was surrounded. He opened his mouth to protest.

"Not a sound from you," Jasper hissed, and moved towards Connor, who backed up against the bins. "Come on, Fatboy, you're coming with us."

Maz and Rowan, two of Jasper's cronies,

grabbed his arms and Connor was frogmarched into the mall. As they passed Jackson's music shop, Casey said, "Wait, what's he going to play? He needs a recorder or flute or something. We can't have him just singing."

The whole group entered the shop, startling the young girl behind the counter. "Have you got any bass guitar strings please?" Jasper asked.

The girl said, "I'll check." She quickly looked in a drawer behind her, just giving Casey enough time to steal a recorder from a bargain display basket by the door. By the time the girl turned back holding several guitar string choices, her shop was empty.

Connor was desperately hoping she would call the mall security team, but no such luck. He could make a run for it, but thought he'd get about two metres. It was ten against one. Again, his eyes were drawn for an instant to the white envelope, now sticking much further out of Jasper's pocket.

Connor found himself standing at the centre of the packed food court in the lower mall, with his eyes fixed on Kelvin's baseball cap at his feet, ready for donations. Hiding their identities with their hoods up, Casey and Jasper rounded up a crowd.

A captive audience at the tables nearby was joined by a semi-circle of inquisitive shoppers. A sweet old lady took out her purse. "I love Christmas!" She dropped a pound coin in the hat saying, "This is to help the little kiddies."

She smiled expectantly at Connor as Jasper announced, "Penguin Massey will now perform some carols. Merry Christmas, everyone!" A small round of applause rippled through the crowd.

"Encore!" shouted the old lady who was enjoying herself enormously. The crowd laughed, and she continued, "Hurry up, I've got to put the sprouts on!" She received an even bigger laugh and curtsied to the crowd.

Connor's eyes flicked to Jasper and his scary smug smile. The bully's laser blue eyes were dancing with expectation, compelling Connor to lift the recorder to his lips. He closed his eyes.

What followed was even worse than his performance as the Pied Piper. It is not an exaggeration to say that not one single recognisable note was played. As people drifted away, a now slightly grumpy old lady bent down to retrieve her pound coin. "That's not Christmas carols. That's just a lot of old noise."

Even Kelvin joined in, and picking up his cap said, "Yeah, just a *lot of old noise*, Fatboy. Useless!"

Jasper stood in front of Connor and shook his head. Then he turned and repeated the action to the few remaining onlookers. The envelope was really sticking out of his pocket now. Connor reached at it to try and bend the top so he could see what was written on it. If he could just see the handwriting, that might... Jasper walked away just as Connor was holding on to the corner, and it slid easily out of his pocket. Connor quickly hid it in his coat before anyone saw. He blew out a couple of quick breaths, unable to comprehend what he'd just managed to do. No one had seen. No one at all.

The gang swept through the food court in a rowdy wave and back up the escalators. Zombie-like, Connor retraced his steps and, unseen, dropped the recorder back in the bargain basket on his way past Jackson's.

Then he walked in a trance towards the cinema and the safety of his friends.

And now he sat with Freddie and Ruby, hidden from the world. Hot tears fell down his face, as Ruby held his shaking hands in hers. She smiled and wiped his crimson cheeks with her hand.

All three quietly reflected on the torment Jasper had inflicted.

"Shall we head home?" asked Freddie.

"No." Connor sniffed. "I want to hear what happened next."

Ruby squeezed Connor's hand again, which encouraged the beginnings of a smile. Connor was so relieved to have got away, he completely forgot to look inside the envelope.

"The plague entered the city, on the 10th June. People were so scared. What was worse, the victim was a servant of one of Pepys friends, Dr Burnet, and to stop the spread he locked himself and his household away so they wouldn't infect anyone.

"Pepys was really upset, because he knew his friend was sacrificing himself. He showed me this weekly sheet that got published called the 'Bills of Mortality' which listed how many people had died and from what causes, and in which parts of London. Every week the numbers just doubled and trebled. It was really taking hold.

"That's when I realised the church bells were ringing non stop, because there were funerals taking place all day at every church. They just couldn't keep up with the number of victims, so funerals stopped, and eventually bodies were just left outside houses. It was all disintegrating so quickly, and everyone was in a real panic."

Freddie, Mingoe and Jack walked round the corner to their favourite hideout, the magnificent but crumbling Whittington Palace. They were safe here, well away from anyone. It had been empty for years and would surely collapse soon if it wasn't repaired. It was four storeys high, and had hundreds of wooden animals carved on exposed timber beams. Dozens of sculpted cats' heads decorated the ceilings, in amongst the gargoyles and crouched goblins, serpents and devils. The boys only ever ventured here during the daylight. Night-time would be too spooky.

The whole of the top floor was one massive rectangular room, reached by a wide rickety staircase. There were leaded glass windows all the way along its sides, and it was completely empty except for a table and fireplace between two doors thirty metres away at the opposite end.

The views from the 'gallery,' as Mingoe called it, were incredible. Not many buildings around them were higher. The Tower of London was on the left, and they could look down into Seething Lane, and beyond to the River Thames. To the right, a wonderful panorama of London opened up all the way to St Paul's, where the huge cathedral and dozens of other churches were the most notable landmarks.

The three of them spent hours up there, talking and day-dreaming, but they were always careful to skirt round the sides of the room, as the floor sagged and creaked scarily when anyone ventured directly across it. There were bench seats under the windows and the boys knelt up on them and surveyed the whole of the city.

"You said you were 'indentured'. What does that mean?"

Mingoe sighed and said, "We were sold to our

masters for a lot of money, and as we work, we are paying back the price they paid for us. So we never see any wages, not a penny. It all disappears into what we owe our masters for buying us in the first place. We are slaves, but by another name, *indentured* slaves. But there is one difference..."

Jack took over. "One day, many years from now, we will be free of our indenture and our masters. We have contracts for thirty-five more years, until we are fifty years old. They say we will have paid our debt by then. Our lives will begin as we become old men, if we are lucky enough to live that long. But until then we must serve our lords, and not ourselves." Jack adjusted the metal collar round his neck which displayed his master's coat of arms. "Inside is my indenture. It's the same as Sir William's copy. That is the only thing equal about us – that we both have identical pieces of paper."

Freddie saw justifiable anger in Mingoe's eyes. "We are fed and housed, and kept healthy, but we can't marry or have children. We can't live a normal life, until we're fifty. Then we are born!"

"And we are the lucky ones," Jack said. "Our brothers and sisters work their days picking cotton, digging ditches and chopping sugarcane, with a white man and a whip standing over them."

"Compared to them, we *are* the lucky ones. We have fancy clothes and embroidered 'kerchiefs, we speak as well as the king, but around our necks hang these metal collars for everyone to see. They show we are not the same. We are *really* not the same. And all the men and women who make us slaves, are the ones who sit in churches and pray for a better world. Well they could start by treating all people as equal and not as possessions – because of the colour of their skin. They made us dance like chained bears, can you imagine that, in the Dolphin Tavern, for all their friends. They…" Mingoe fell quiet.

Jack continued, "That was one of the worst days of our lives, being laughed at like animals. They treat their horses and dogs better. We won't ever forget that." A silence fell.

"But, the 12th August 1700, that is when I will be born," recovered Jack. "You?" He directed to Mingoe.

"Not until 11th January 1701," whispered his friend. "Then I will be known by my real name, Kwanza. It means 'first fruit', because I was my father's first child. Until then, I am just Mingoe." He bowed his head and a long silence followed.

"Well, you can come and work for me until you are free," joked Jack.

Mingoe laughed. "Never! You would make me dig holes twelve hours a day." The two young men smiled gently at each other, and then lost themselves again in their thoughts. Freddie sat speechless and mortified.

"Talking of digging holes…" The silence was interrupted again by Jack, pointing at St Olave's churchyard below them, where another series of graves were being filled with linen-wrapped bodies. The ground level had risen dramatically as more burials took place, and now it was three feet higher than before. Coffins were a thing of the past as there was no spare wood to make them.

"Pepys told me they've dug four huge pits at Moore Fields and put fifteen hundred bodies in each," said Freddie. "And five more at St Giles because the churchyards are full."

"We've got to find a way to help," Jack mused.

The wailing chant of 'Bring out your dead' wafted upwards on the warm air. The boys stared at the streets below, where men shrouded in thick coats, gauntlets and face coverings loaded bodies onto carts until they could carry no more. Tolling bells sounded all around them, and the temptation was to stay hidden in this safe place, but their evening duties called. They would have to leave planning their freedom from slavery, and helping the plague sufferers, for another day.

Chapter 7

At the end of June, the king departed London for Hampton Court.

"It's a fine thing our sovereign king is safe, but where *he* leads, others follow," said Pepys as he strode into Garraway's coffeehouse by the Exchange. "Meet me in the quadrangle as the bell strikes twelve," he added over his shoulder and handed Freddie several pamphlets for safekeeping. *With the amount of bell-ringing around, it'll be a miracle if I can pick out 12 o'clock,* Freddie thought.

Looking at the pages, he saw that the king had indeed gone, and as Boghurst predicted, almost the entire medical profession followed suit. Another story said only one in three shops was now open, and only one customer was allowed in at a time. All coins were to be placed in a dish of vinegar on the counter to disinfect them of the pestilence. The quarantine period was set at forty days, after which if your family was showing no signs of illness, the street door could be opened and normal life resumed. Another article said, "This will exceed the outbreak of 1625 when 40,000 souls perished." It blamed the exceptional spring and summer temperatures.

Then news Freddie wasn't expecting. "The cats must go to the dogs." All cats and dogs were to be killed as it was thought by some in authority that they were responsible for spreading the disease.

"But that was the worst thing they could have done," Freddie explained. "I've been reading all about it since I got back, and the plague was carried by fleas on black rats, and killing all the cats and dogs took away their major predators. So when the rats died, the fleas transferred to whatever else was moist and warm, and they just multiplied in the dark backstreets during the hot summer."

"So, I had an hour to kill in the Royal Exchange. It was amazing. Around the courtyard were two floors of shops, with statues of all the kings and queens of England, including my new best mate Charlie!" Freddie smiled with the others.

"It was full of rich men doing deals, and fine ladies parading about with servants carrying dresses and birdcages and all sorts. Actually the men spent just as much in the tailors and wig makers.

"As I was looking at musical instruments in a window, all of a sudden this crazy man jumped up behind me and started shouting and waving his hands. He was just spouting nonsense and spitting and dribbling. He had greasy hair and wild eyes and stinking rag clothes. Everyone stopped and stared. I was pressed up against the shop door trying to get away from him. Then he stuffed a piece of paper down my shirtfront, and swore at me as he ran away. I was petrified. I didn't know if he had the plague or not. It was really frightening. I took out the scrunched-up note and it said, 'You are not wanted here. Return to your own kind. Or the purple beast will get you.' It was in really shaky writing, like someone scrawling with their wrong hand. And guess what? It was in turquoise ink. How weird is that?"

"No way," said Connor.

"You're joking?" added Ruby. So what did the first letter say, the Latin letter?"

Pepys appeared wearing a new black frockcoat and breeches, like he'd just stepped out of a shop window. He was waddling along because the material was so stiff, and he had a giant wig on, nearly double the size of his old one.

"Well, Fred m'boy, how do I look? Will I pass for

a courtier in m'new suit? Will the ladies think me irresistible?"

"Yes, sir, you look *amazing*," Freddie lied, actually thinking he resembled a smiling pig tottering about in high heels.

"*Amazing!* I like that. Now, who shall I *amaze* first?" Pepys slipped a silver penny into Freddie's hand for his flattering compliment. "I have to see the Mayor so take my old things home and wait for me."

Freddie raced back and found the Latin note in his library and took it to a church away from Seething Lane.

"I thought that a priest would be the best person to read Latin, but I couldn't risk the reverend Mills from St Olave's over the road, just in case it said something dodgy about me or Pepys.

"I went to St Botolph's on Thames Street, and told this really old priest that a lawyer whose Latin was poor had sent me and he needed a translation."

"A lawyer who doesn't read Latin? Well it doesn't surprise me in these ungodly times. But lawyers need to pay for favours."

"I only have a silver penny, sir, will that do?"

"Let me see the length of it? What strange ink! A foreign hand, I've no doubt. Let's see. 'Beware the stranger in your house, he is an exploratorum.'

Exploratorum? Let me think. Yes! that means spy — *spy* is the word. 'He is a spy who is working for the Gallico.' Now *Gallico* means French. It goes on, 'Guard well your naval secrets, for he seeks advantage of you. Signed *'Amica'*, which means 'a friend'.

"Well, well, well. No wonder your master needed that translated. How exciting. Your penny if you please, towards the relief of the pestilence. Good day, young man."

Freddie's mind raced, and passing a street vendor selling hot pies outside a cook shop, he fed the turquoise note into the flames that warmed the food. He watched it burn, *exploratorum* the final word to be consumed by the fire. He felt like James Bond. *Who's sending these turquoise letters?* He would have to find out, and quickly.

Soon after, Pepys returned from his meeting with the mayor.

"Sir John Lawrence conducts his business from a glass box, would you believe? He's had it made. Won't touch hands or breathe the same air as the rest of us. He conducts the city's business from behind four glass walls for fear of contagion. He's a wise man. No one shakes hands anymore or kisses their neighbour in greeting. We live in perilous times, young Fred." A knock at the door found Billy Jenks standing there with news for Pepys.

"Well what is it, boy?"

"Beg pardon, sir, a kind lady says your baker has died of the plesti sance, the—"

"*Pestilence*," helped Freddie.

"Yeah! *That!* She said to thank you for your custom, and to arrange for your bread elsewhere."

"Goodness me, would you believe it? First my butcher, then my brewer, and now my baker. The world is getting smaller. Here's a farthing for your trouble, boy. Freddie, take these coins to the widow, and then this letter to Mr Boghurst. My thanks to him are overdue." He stared out of the window. "What a great shame. Where will I get my bread now?" Not for the first time, Freddie thought Pepys insensitive and selfish. "It's all about him," he heard Uncle Patrick say in his head.

Billy Jenks showed them the baker's house. Along with the Red Cross on the door and '*Lord have mercy upon us*' written above, there was a simple message that read, 'No more bread – the baker's dead.' It was a shame it rhymed because it made the news appear trivial or funny.

The quartet of boys called from the centre of the narrow alley and a woman appeared at an upstairs window. Recognising Billy, she opened it slowly.

Freddie said, "Mr Samuel Pepys says to tell you he is so sorry to hear about your husband, and to give you these coins to soothe your troubled predicament." Mingoe and Jack had helped with the words, having heard them used the day before.

"Tell him thank you, but keep them. Coins won't soothe what's in this house. The dead, the dying, the mad and incurable, we're all locked in together. No coins are going to help. Only in death will we find our cure. May God bless you, and spare you this living hell! My husband had a big bag of coins but that didn't save him. You take those coins and drink a toast to us on our journey." And with that she shut the window.

The four boys stood and bowed their heads respectfully before silently walking along the alley where every third or fourth house was now showing a red cross.

"How much is there?" asked Billy Jenks, wiping his nose vigorously. Freddie counted.

"It's four pounds, well just over actually."

"Cor! Jus' like that, he can splash four quid on his baker. What must that be like?" sniffed Billy.

"Let's share it four ways," said Freddie. "A pound each."

"What?" gasped Billy. "That's a year's money in one hit. My ma will be beside herself." He stared in wonder as the coins were divided, with the extra going to Billy by general agreement. He wiped tears of joy from his face with one sleeve, and his runny nose with the other, then smiled. "Got somefing in my eye, that's all."

"Keep it safe, Billy, until you get to your mother," advised Jack. "Go straight home and tell her your news."

"Shouldn't we give it back to Pepys though?" said Billy suddenly. He had a point. The quartet fell silent as they thought over the problem.

"It was a gift from Pepys to the baker's wife, and then the baker's wife to us, so, no! I don't think so. I think it's fair to share it. I'm going to spend mine fighting the plague," Freddie said.

Billy Jenks skipped off towards Alsatia, promising to tell them how his ma took the news.

The others made for Boghurst's shop outside the city walls in the packed streets just north of the Grand Piazza in Covent Garden. Freddie couldn't believe his eyes. It was almost the same as when he visited on a school trip two years ago when his class had eaten their packed lunches, watching jugglers and buskers. It was a great feeling to be away from the narrow dark streets and into some light.

A shrouded figure darted into a church and out of sight. Freddie stopped in his tracks.

"Are you all right?" asked Mingoe. "You look like you've seen a ghost."

"No, I'm fine," he blustered.

Moments later the boys stood outside Boghurst's shop. A sign said 'Strictly one at a time' and Freddie entered cautiously. Shelves lined the walls, packed with dozens of labelled jars of medicines, dried plants, herbs and pastes. Freddie's eyes picked out aniseed, wormwood and opium. At the far end of the shop a high counter contained ladles and spatulas, scales and measures. Even tea, coffee and chocolate were on sale, but at sky-high prices, and a pleasant mixed spice smell welcomed Freddie.

Boghurst emerged from a back room when he heard the doorbell.

"Can I help?" he asked quietly.

"Yes, sir, I have a letter from my master, Samuel Pepys."

"Yes, I thought I recognised you. Your name?"

"Freddie Malone."

"Thank you, Freddie. Has your master's headache disappeared – the one he acquired from too much wine?"

"Yes, sir, only just. He has headaches quite often."

Boghurst laughed and accepted the letter after putting gloves on. He smiled apologetically. "You understand I'm sure?"

"Yes, sir. I was wondering how to help? If there is anything we can do? He indicated Mingoe and Jack at the window.

"Ah! Angels of Mercy, well let me see." He beckoned them inside. "Whilst most of my colleagues flee the city, you brave boys wish to help, is that right?" He ushered them through to his workroom. Books lined one wall and he pulled a pamphlet from a shelf. "Look at this and tell me what you think."

On the front cover was a drawing of a man wearing

a floor-length cloak and heavy boots. He had gauntlets nearly to the elbow, and a separate cowl which covered his neck and shoulders and made a hood, held in place by a wide-brimmed hat. But the most striking thing was the mask the man wore. A complete facemask with cutouts for the eyes, and a huge beak that stuck out of the front. It was a truly alarming sight. All three boys recoiled.

"That's the only way to help," Boghurst told them. "Protect yourself and dispense aid to the dying, and the poor souls locked up with them.

"Why do you need the beak?" asked Jack.

"It's full of herbs and sweet-smelling dried flowers to stop the desperate stench of death from reaching you. I can tell you from experience, there is not another smell in this world that is worse."

The three boys looked at the pamphlet, then at each other, before nervously nodding agreement.

Freddie said, "You have three volunteers, sir. Tell us what to do."

Maybe, finally, he had found out why he was here.

Chapter 8

"Getting clothes is no problem," Boghurst told them. "A great friend, Sir Michael Povey, recently died. He ran a large emporium, which sold everything the Thames boatmen use to keep out the weather, except for facemasks which we shall make. His family have fled to Dorsetshire, leaving me to watch over the shop. They are rich enough to spare the clothes you'll need. I recommend you change every three days and then burn what you've worn. We'll make the masks from old leather garments, and I have the necessary herbs for your beaks."

"Thank you very much, Mr Boghurst," said Freddie.

"Call me Boggy, all my friends do." His kind face crinkled into a smile.

"Thank you, err, Boggy. You said getting outfitted wasn't the problem, meaning something else is?"

"Yes. It's hard to describe man's greed. There are gangs, I'm sure you're aware, that prey on the sick and the dying. They terrorise them, charging prices for food way above the decent level one might expect. A penny loaf will cost five times that, and no doubt be stale and inedible when supplied. Water will be rank and dirty. Beer mixed so weak, and costing ten times a normal draught. The poor victims have no choice but to pay, and these thugs know it. But that's not the worst." Boggy shook his head and scratched his chin. "Worse, *far* worse than that, is their newfound habit of using children to plunder the homes of the dead. They have always used boys to steal and pilfer. But now they tie them to a rope and send them into a plague house to bring out all they can carry. How long can a child withstand the disease when set that task? And if they refuse, they are whipped 'til they comply. I don't need to go on, but it's up to people like us to expose that behaviour and to give some comfort to those forsaken souls in their final days, before they pass to the next life."

For a while they were all lost in their own thoughts, then for the rest of the afternoon they sewed their headgear. They cut up an old leather coat for facemasks, and created sturdy beaks on wooden frames that were easily emptied and refilled. Adjustments were made and straps attached to keep them in place.

"Which of your master's has a new wig? An ounce

of flaxen locks has suddenly dropped from twelve shillings to eight as there's so much. Where do you think it's coming from? There are devils who shear off the hair of corpses before they're thrown in their graves. They sell the tresses to fancy makers who still charge the usual high price for wigs. But they pass on infected hair, and kill themselves and their customers for a profit they won't be alive to spend. How deadly stupid." Freddie thought of Pepys's new wig. He must wash it in his antiseptic.

"I will give you the rear door key of Povey's Emporium. An alley near the Tower allows you access. But make sure no one sees you and lock the door behind you. Report to me on your progress or for fresh herbs."

On the journey to Povey's, the streets felt eerily quiet. Those who were dying were locked away, and those still alive were scared of venturing out. Carts continually rumbled along, with bodies piled high, and shouts of 'Bring out your dead' rang out, mixing with the constant tolling of church bells. In 1665, the job of bell-ringer seemed to be the most secure profession in London.

The removal of bodies was originally undertaken at night hoping not to alarm people, but now the carts carried their dreadful cargo around the clock. The sight of once-healthy citizens, now piled like logs, had become so common that Freddie was almost immune to the horrors.

Some bodies were even left by their front doors, with many more locked inside, with no relatives left alive to carry them out.

The boys turned east into Thames Street from Pudding Lane as it was wider and nearer the river, hoping a breeze might waft away the ever present stench. With the packed warehouses on their right and the rich merchants' houses on their left, they talked through their plan.

"I can use my pound to buy bread and cheese and whatever else people want, and we can pick a few streets and sell things at the normal price. Then, we can buy more stock, and so on," said Freddie.

"Look!" Jack whispered. Two hundred metres in front of them was a gang pulling handcarts loaded with candlesticks and carpets, paintings and fancy clothes. They were working the many grand houses on the left of the street with red crosses on the doors.

Freddie gasped as he saw two men pull a rope, and a small boy was dragged from a house with a box laden with heavy silver pieces. The contents were tipped into the cart and the boy sent back in to gather more. Two lads were being alternated, and no sooner had one emerged than the other was forced back in.

Freddie gasped. They instantly recognised the distinctive orange top. Wilting under the weight of his box, the boy poured its contents into the cart:

clocks, cutlery, silver and gold. Then the boy was sent back in. Slowly the house was emptied. A neighbour complained but was threatened by one of the gang with a cudgel, and retreated indoors.

Freddie, Mingoe and Jack hid in the doorway of St Botolph's. The gang didn't touch anything except the cart handles and the rope ends that held the boys. They had long given up the business of selling food and drink. This was far more profitable. They were getting richer with every thieving minute.

The small boys emerged again and the carts were full. They picked up speed and pulled the bewildered children behind them.

"The Packers!" mouthed Mingoe.

"Their store must be around here," Freddie whispered.

Both carts turned right towards the river. "Yes, look! They're turning down to Dice Quay," said Mingoe, and led Jack and Freddie to the shaded doorway of the deserted Dolphin Tavern, for a perfect view.

Outside the warehouse stood the huge man who was chewing meat from a bone and shouting orders.

"Put coins and jewellery in the vinegar bucket and rinse clothes in the milky liquid. Dip the large silver and gold treasures in the stone basin, then carry them inside."

Next to him sat two women on a bench. The younger one had a mean face and no teeth. She absent-mindedly threw a thin knife into the ground, picked it up, wiped the blade on her dress and repeated the action. Next to her was a formidable matron who sat smoking a long clay pipe. She had waist length, grey, greasy hair under a mop cap. Her face was expressionless. Occasionally she gestured for something to be presented for her inspection. Freddie was just close enough to catch what was said.

"Take those 'ropers' out for another run after you've had a tot. Thirsty work, I shouldn't wonder." She spat in the dirt.

"Yes, Ma, thirsty but profitable, extremely profitable."

"Bob, get me a dress next time, a nice blue one," uttered the toothless girl.

"What? You think a blue dress'll turn you into a lady, Aggie Packer?" joked one of the gang. Suddenly, her knife flashed into his shirtsleeve, pinning his arm against the wooden doorpost.

"Aahh!" he cried. "I was only joking."

"It's only a nick, Travers," barked Aggie. "Next time, I won't spare you. Now get on with Ma's orders." The man unpinned his grazed arm under their hawk-like gaze. Old Ma Packer removed her pipe and spat in his direction. Turning to go she instructed Bob, "Feed the ropers. By the look of 'em they've only got one run left. Line up another couple for tomorrow."

"Yes, Ma. You heard her, get me two more and

bring 'em down tonight." Travers ran off, no doubt glad to be out of Aggie's range.

Soon, all had disappeared into the warehouse except Bob who asked the two 'ropers', "Who's hungry then?" They were tethered to a post and they held out their hands, making whimpering sounds. Bob threw two chunks of bread and they scrabbled to pick them up. But he had deliberately thrown them short, impossible to reach. The warehouse slammed shut cutting off Bob Packer's cruel laugh.

Without thinking, Freddie broke from cover and charged straight for the bread, which he kicked towards the boys. They dropped to the ground and began eating ravenously. He went to the post where their ropes were tethered and using his multi-tool, he hacked at the fibres and made swift work of releasing them.

But they stayed put. Freddie shooed them away. "Run! Quick! While you've got the chance." But as he neared the boy with the orange top, he could see his eyes were glazed. He was bewildered. The second boy seemed more alert and Freddie managed to get him to stagger away, pulling his friend and clutching the bread. They lurched down the slope to the river, and were last seen scrambling along the muddy shore line.

Freddie raced back to Mingoe and Jack and the three shared a triumphant smile. Now they had an enemy to fight. Now they had a cause. For the second time today Freddie felt he was going to make a difference.

Aggie, Bob and Old Ma Packer didn't know what they had unleashed by their cowardice and greed. The Angels of Mercy were up and running and the next stop was Povey's Emporium.

The actual name of the shop was 'Sir Michael Povey's All-Weather Nautical Emporium'. They slipped easily into the yard at the back of the shop, and the first thing they saw was a four wheeled cart which exactly suited their needs. Whilst Jack checked it worked and cleared it of debris, Freddie and Mingoe entered the shop.

In no time, they were back out with three outfits each, enough for at least a week of missions. Coats, hats, hoods, boots and gauntlets, as well as knives, rope, candles and matches. They carefully locked up and checked the coast was clear. They wheeled the cart over Tower Hill, and hid their equipment inside the deserted gatehouse of Whittington Palace.

They were in time for their evening chores, which for Freddie involved transporting Elizabeth and the household to a friend of Pepys's in Woolwich, where they would be safe.

Pepys declared, "We will see you to kind Mr Sheldon's house, and then Freddie and I will face the pestilence here. We will knock it on the head and send it packing, and you will all be back with us in no time."

Brave words, thought Freddie. But his mission alongside Mingoe and Jack would begin tomorrow.

The 'Angels of Mercy' might not exactly knock the plague on the head, but they would provide some much-needed comfort and help to people who were desperate, frightened and alone.

Chapter 9

"Those poor boys," said Ruby. "Sending them into those infected houses! What happened to them?" Freddie didn't answer but let the thought hang in the air. It was getting dark and the high street was packed with frantic shoppers zigzagging with armfuls of bags. With three days until Christmas, the panic and excitement was building.

Freddie and Ruby stretched as they stood, and pressed their noses against the glass, studying the ant-like movements below.

"Guys! Err, guys, help. Help, HELP!"

"What is it?" Ruby turned to see Connor's left arm outstretched towards her. There, on the inside, midway between elbow and wrist was a huge purple mark. The three gasped and looked at each other in a panic. It was shaped like a massive flowering rose head, and Freddie mouthed, "*Pestilential token.*" Connor rolled up his other sleeve, whilst Freddie and Ruby stood horrified.

"I've got the plague!"

But suddenly Ruby was smiling. "Connor, look at your carrier bag."

"What are you laughing at? It's not funny. I've got the plague."

"No you haven't. Look at your bag, Connor!" Freddie pointed.

"Whaaaatt?" Straight away Connor saw the blackcurrant juice leaking from a split. The three of them dissolved in fits of relieved giggles, but, unseen by his friends, a serious look crossed Freddie's face. It wasn't impossible, was it? With him travelling between the past and present... what if...? He pushed the thought from his mind.

Returning to the others from the bin and putting on his things to go home, Connor put his hand in his coat to get his gloves. He pulled out the envelope he'd lifted from Jasper's back pocket. "Wow, I'd forgotten all about this! You open it, Freddie, I'll only mess it up."

"No. You found it, it's your honour."

Connor examined the plain white envelope and held it up to the light. "There's something in it.'

"All right, Sherlock! OPEN IT!" urged Ruby. Connor cautiously ran his finger under the flap and looked inside. He looked up at his friends as he pulled out a wad of bank notes. They gasped for the second time in a minute. Freddie examined the envelope. He half expected to see the colour turquoise somewhere.

"Thirty, Forty, Fifty!" said Ruby, counting for the second time.

"Maybe it's a Christmas present or something, from a granddad?" Freddie offered.

Connor shook his head. "No, it was for them all, because Kelvin tried to grab it before Jasper put it away. Then the old man pointed at them all, and they all nodded. That's when Casey saw me."

"Well let's spend... I mean *look after* it for them until we find out more," smiled Ruby.

"Good plan, RooBeeRoo!" Freddie teased.

"Oi! Only my mum gets away with that."

Freddie pulled a mock 'sorry' face.

"I'll forgive you if you carry on with the adventure," Ruby said.

Freddie looked at his phone. "OK, I've got an hour." Connor was already sitting back down with his coat off, unwrapping blackcurrant-soaked sweets, which gave his fingers the plague now as well.

Freddie had his work cut out in the morning looking after Pepys and doing his other chores. Pepys complained his oysters weren't fresh, but relented when he saw how hard Freddie was working. "You've got the day to yourself, Fred. I'm on Navy duties. But I shall need you this evening for the Royal Society."

Taking a bucket, some rags and his bottle of antiseptic, he called for Mingoe and Jack who promised to join him at Whittington Palace after their work was done. As he waited, Freddie cleaned the cart and containers with his strong solution, carefully dressed in all his kit, minus the hat and mask. Not long after he finished, his friends arrived.

The first stop was Lombard Street market, nearing the end of its morning session, and a time when bargains were available as stallholders wanted to get home for lunch and a sleep before opening up again in late afternoon. Mingoe was by far the best at bargaining, and even played two bakers off against each other, getting fifteen loaves for the price of twelve from a happy man who could now go home early. Jack suggested buying the less attractive chunks of cheese from the end of the blocks that were half price, and soon their cart was full. They stood on the corner of Philpot Lane and Fanchurch Street, and put the finishing touches to their outfits.

They had specifically chosen this street because it was full of houses with red crosses, but no one answered at the first four doors. At the fifth an elderly woman's face appeared at a peep window. She took one look at the masked boys and screamed, "The devil's come for my children!" And she slammed the window in fear. They altered their method after that! Freddie went ahead in the middle of the street, without his mask, shouting, "Bread, cheese, candles, matches, at market prices!" Mingoe and Jack followed with the cart and gradually started to sell their goods to the trapped occupants. At first everyone was alarmed to see the beaked masks but Freddie explained, "It's to protect us from the pestilence, to make sure we can come back tomorrow."

"My dying wish is to feed on a sprat," said a pale young man speaking from an upstairs room.

"We will do our best, sir. Same time tomorrow?"

"If I survive the night, God willing," said the man wistfully. Mingoe and Jack left the food purchased on windowsills, with the coins for payment placed in a bowl of vinegar at its side.

House after house in the short street revealed someone desperately trying to stay alive and look after those inside, or someone in the early throes of the disease with a haunted expression in their eyes. Most disturbing were those in the final stages, when madness had taken hold, and their rantings were at their most frightening.

After that first afternoon, they had witnessed enough heartache to last a lifetime. Some people couldn't speak they were so upset. Others were helplessly grateful for the kindness the boys were showing. Others swore and told them to take their charity elsewhere. One angry man even wished the plague on Freddie, but the majority were extremely thankful to have some fresh food and not at the ridiculous prices charged by the gangs and watchmen.

It was a cumbersome process, exchanging goods and money. It took time to accomplish safely. But it gave an opportunity to tell news of the outside world. People enquired about the spread of the disease, the war at sea, and the royal family. Freddie promised news sheets and pamphlets on their round tomorrow, and beer. A lot of people requested beer. After an hour, and with very little stock left, they stood outside a splendid mansion opposite the alley to Turners' Hall. Alconbury House.

As Freddie drew breath to launch into his sales pitch, a well-groomed, elderly man with long silver hair waved from a wide bay window to the left of the large front door. He nodded a greeting to Freddie, and was not at all perturbed by the sight of Mingoe and Jack as their beaks followed into view. He had a noble bearing and stood strong and upright, showing a keen interest in the carts. He opened a window slightly and stood back again, projecting his voice with an easy authority so he could be heard.

"Good day to you three gallant gentlemen. My daughters and I have been getting extremely excited at your approach along our forgotten lane." Then, almost like swans gliding over a lake, five young girls aged between ten and twenty, gathered either side of him looking eagerly at the three boys below.

"I see trade has been brisk. My neighbours must be hungry. Can I purchase what you have left, and entreat you to come to us tomorrow with fresh stocks. If I give you this golden guinea, would you return to this house daily until…?" For the first time his calm authority deserted him and he looked lovingly left and right at his girls.

"Of course, it will be an honour," said Mingoe. "We can come again tomorrow, and we'll start with your house."

"Thank you, that is most kind. Allow me to introduce myself. My name is Sir Bradley Roast and these are my five daughters, Trinity, Mercy, Charity, Faith and Patience." With each introduction a girl bobbed a curtsy and looked back coyly into the street. "Their mother, Constance, has… has been taken from us. One of the first to depart in this parish. We think she must have contracted the disease at church in June. 'A great pity,' she said before she died, 'as the sermon was so poor!'" The man braved a smile, before his face briefly crumpled with the enormous pain of his loss.

"We have been in quarantine for thirty days, with ten to go until we can escape into fresh air. We long for our Devon farm where we will go and be safe."

"So, just over a week to go, sir?" Freddie said. It was rare for people to last this long once the pestilence was in the house.

"Indeed, ten short days and then the watchman who normally stands guard here will turn our key and we will walk to freedom."

"Where's the watchman now?"

"Spending his profits, no doubt. Ha! What do you take for a penny loaf?"

"A penny, sir. No more, no less," said Jack.

"Well our watchman, one Curtis Bran, charges sixpence. *Six*, would you believe? He will be mightily displeased we have a new supplier, so please watch the watchman." He smiled at his own joke, as did his daughters.

"Your guinea will enable us to buy a cart each, Sir Bradley, and we will serve three times as many vict... err, people."

"I'm so glad. What is money? What are paintings and fine clothes when faced with a sentence like this? A guinea is the very least I can do to triple the houses you can help. Now what have you left this fine July day?"

The last two loaves and chunks of cheese were placed on a tray which the eldest girl left on the wide windowsill, and she dropped the guinea into the vinegar and smiled gratefully into Mingoe's eyes, the only part of his body visible in his protective costume.

"Trinity, please take our feast to the dining room and serve on our best plates. I don't see why we should let standards slip, do you? Forgive me, gentlemen, your names? So I can write about you in my journal?"

"Freddie, sir."

"Mingoe."

"And Jack, Sir Bradley. We will see you tomorrow."

"Yes indeed you will. Indeed you will."

As they trundled their empty cart away they removed their headgear and turned into Little Eastcheap. A sweaty and grotesque man in a blue watchman's coat raced past them with his spear trailing after him. He grunted suspiciously at the boys and a minute later took up his villainous guard outside Alconbury House.

So, Freddie had yet another mission. How best to make sure this greedy man got what he deserved preoccupied all their minds on the journey back.

Pepys was rushing as usual and only interested in his own news, so Freddie wasn't even asked about his movements. Tonight's first lecture at the Royal Society was from Boghurst, or Boggy as Freddie now knew him. Freddie hid at the back of the hall, listening intently to his new friend, who went on to say, "My lords, gentlemen, I give you the figures for June where, due to plague, six hundred souls departed this life. And for July so far over four thousand have followed – at least a six-fold increase. And this doesn't take into account the falsehood of the figures declared by the searchers, who reduce the numbers for their own gain. We can add at least a third to find the real tally. The churches must mobilise. Praying is all well and good, but it won't stop the spread of the pestilence.

"Gentlemen, superstition abounds. People are spending small fortunes on fake cures. Some profiteers say that learning a list of lucky numbers will halt the disease, and they charge highly for their disclosure. Rubbish! Some people sell pictures of stars or serpents to ward off the plague. It will cost you a pretty penny now, but will ultimately cost you your life as these fakeries will not work. Fresh air, clean water, sanitation and the eradication of the fetid alleys and passages of our godforsaken city are the only cure for this beast."

There was a murmur of approval from the great minds present, and Boggy continued, "And, gentlemen, beware your new wig. It may well come from the scalp of an unfortunate who has been shorn even as she is lowered into the ground. Mark well my words."

Freddie could see Pepys's face redden with panic. On his head perched his magnificent purchase, but what *did* it contain? A death sentence? All the way home in the coach he fretted until Freddie suggested the wig was washed in a strong solution he'd had recommended by Boghurst himself.

"If you would, Fred, and set it away for a month or

two, maybe longer. I'll be happy to wear my old ones. After all the king and court are far off and won't see me in this state."

"Of course, sir," said Freddie.

"In fact, Fred, let's burn the thing. I don't like it anyway. I feel like I'm wearing a bird's nest, it's so uncomfortable. And the colour doesn't suit me either. Burn it when we get home."

"Of course, sir," Freddie smiled.

Chapter 10

Over the last week of July the boys perfected their deliveries. They now had a cart each and filled barrels with fresh water in Cornhill every morning, and collected unwanted pamphlets at coffeehouses en route to Lombard Street, where competition to serve the boys was now fierce. It was deemed good luck, as if it would ensure the plague would pass them by. Soon they could get twenty loaves for the price of twelve. They bought fish and cheese at half price and as much beer as they could carry. The traders were happy that they were doing their bit to help. The plague had, after all, touched all their families.

One day as they approached Sir Bradley's house, the vile watchman Curtis Bran stepped out of the dark alley opposite. He twisted his ferocious spear.

"The 'Angels of Mercy' are you?" He spat. "Ha! You

look like devils to me in your hoods and beaks. Show yerselves, you cowards. You rob me of m'living. This is *my* lane, and Roast is *my* customer. I found him fair and square."

The boys dropped the handles of their carts and stood in front of them protectively. Freddie opened his mouth to speak but was stopped by Mingoe and Jack who pushed him gently backwards. Still in their hoods and beaks they advanced on Bran who brandished his spear as protection.

"Now, you dogs, Leave Philpot Lane to me, or else!"

But that was the last intelligible sentence they heard from him. Mingoe and Jack started to stamp and dance, gesturing wildly, and chanting intensely at increasing volume as they rotated around the confused man. He thrust his spear at Mingoe and Jack, which they easily avoided. With each lunge they upped their tempo and exaggerated their strange invented moves. The watchman panicked and his aggression turned to a desperate cry to be spared from the pestilence. Still the boys circled, never letting Curtis Bran rest as he spun and dizzied himself, expecting to be attacked and infected. But they didn't lay a finger on him. In the end he threw down his weapon, offered them his purse, and fled screaming into the distance as fast as his short legs could carry him.

Mingoe and Jack collapsed in a giggling breathless

heap and retrieved the spilled coins, whilst Freddie, still laughing, turned towards Alconbury House. He stiffened and went silent. At the window stood Sir Bradley, with *four* daughters.

Trinity, the eldest girl, was nowhere to be seen.

In the days that followed, the boys noticed the distance between customers vastly increased, so they broadened their mission, taking in a bigger area. Watchmen and searchers were now scarce, and the 'Angels of Mercy' had the streets to themselves, except for the carts removing bodies.

The boys were now well known and they were told about small pockets of survivors who needed help, and their example rubbed off on several nearby churches, who copied their methods.

Individual gang members shadowed them twice. Freddie thought they might be checking which houses were empty in order to send in the 'ropers', so they varied their routes and timings, hoping to wrong-foot them. They warned the stallholders at market that the Packers might try to interfere, and the traders assured them they would help if they did.

Whatever route their daily mission took, they made sure Philpot Lane was always first. More and more households succumbed, until one day Alconbury House was the only dwelling in the whole lane with anyone alive inside.

Every day Sir Bradley would stand at the bay window, and his remaining daughters would glide to his side. Mingoe and Jack removed their masks here, but still a safe distance was kept as they talked. Trinity had fallen seven days short of the quarantine. So close to freedom! Now they had to start the long count again, but no one was pretending anything other than a negative outcome was going to result.

Sir Bradley was fascinated by Mingoe and Jack, and wanted to hear about how they found themselves in London. Mingoe told of his father's terrible journey to Barbados, packed in a slave ship. Jack then explained their indenture to their masters, and Sir Bradley shook his head in disgust.

A great bond grew between them all. His daughters, especially young Patience, asked lots of questions, and Sir Bradley often had to intervene, "Now, dear, let these fine gentlemen about their business. We cannot be selfish and keep them all to ourselves, much as we may want to."

Sometimes Billy Jenks joined them on their rounds, but complained that he couldn't wipe his nose and his eyes watered because of the pungent herbs in his beak. He took it off for a while, but soon replaced it as the stench in Finch Lane nearly finished him off. "Smells like the devil's guts have rotted." He didn't complain about the herbs again.

Freddie looked at the time on his phone. "I've got to go, sorry, guys."

"Tell us what happened next. We can walk with you, please?" asked Connor.

"All right, but I can't be late. Not tonight. Finnegan would kill me."

"What happened to Sir Bradley and his girls?" asked Ruby as they emerged onto the busy pavement. Freddie looked at them both and as they set off, he continued.

"Well, we carried on delivering, but a week after Trinity died, Mercy was missing. Nothing was said. Sir Bradley just shook his head. Then, four days later, Faith went and Charity soon after. The pain on Sir Bradley's face showed that he was too upset to talk. None of us knew what to say. Now it was just him and Patience at the window.

"One day she said, 'It's Father's birthday on Saturday. Please could we have some meat as my present to him?' She shakily produced a silver coin."

"Of course. We will bring anything you want. What is your favourite?" Freddie asked Sir Bradley as brightly as possible.

"You are very kind, a hint of lamb or beef. It's been so long since I've tasted either. Just a small cut mind, as there is only..." His voice trembled a moment.

"Neither of us have great appetites anymore I'm afraid. What a thoughtful present, Patience dearest. Thank you."

The day before his birthday the boys delivered a piece of the finest beefsteak and as they approached, Sir Bradley was already in place. He was in full military dress uniform, with a broad blue diagonal sash, sword, hat and boots.

But, Patience didn't join him.

He very slowly shook his head and moved to the window to take the meat that was wrapped in a muslin cloth.

"No news today thank you, gentlemen. I am not in the mood to hear about this world. I must concentrate on the next. Although, if you have beer with you, I would be very keen to purchase a great deal of that." He fetched two glass jugs, and Mingoe filled them with the thick brown ale. "Good, that should send me to sleep nicely. Thank you, gentlemen. In case, for any reason I am not here tomorrow, this letter is for you, for the three of you. I will leave it this side of the glass, under the tile here. I wore new gloves as I wrote, so I hope it is free from infection. Please read it… when you feel the time is appropriate." He paused, and looked skywards. "It seems to be another glorious August day. How lovely. Good luck on your rounds, gentlemen. Thank you, and farewell."

And with that Sir Bradley slipped away from view.

As they turned into Little Eastcheap Mingoe broke the terrible silence.

"Did you see his neck? There was a huge purple mark above his collar." The three boys sat in silence on their carts and knew they had made their last delivery to Philpot Lane.

From the cover of a sheltered doorway along the street, a shrouded figure watched with interest. A cruel smile danced on his thin lips.

Arriving at 10 Normandy Avenue, Connor, Ruby and Freddie stood in silence outside his house, as if at a vigil for Sir Bradley and his daughters.

"I'm sorry, Connor," said Freddie.

"What?"

"I'm sorry I wasn't there to help you in the mall with Jasper."

"That's OK," Connor replied, his mind still in Philpot Lane.

"Me too, Conman," said Ruby, hugging him briefly. "See you tomorrow."

"Yeah," the boys answered in unison as Ruby disappeared into the house next door.

Finnegan and Kathleen emerged from Freddie's, in coats, scarves, gloves and hats ready to go out.

"Hurry up!" shouted Finnegan at top volume. "We'll be late for the carol service. Come on! Leave the fat boy alone, we've got to go!"

The boys exchanged looks and Freddie went inside to change, leaving Finnegan glaring at Connor. Connor stared back. He didn't know where he found the nerve to do it, but he looked defiantly into the old man's grey eyes. He even lifted his chin a little before turning to go. *That'll show him*, Connor thought. Then he turned and concentrated hard on not slipping on the frosty pavement. That would totally destroy his 'cool', but he successfully disappeared out of sight. Mission accomplished.

The cold December night chilled the sweat on his forehead as he trudged home, keeping to the shadows. Always hiding. Always on the lookout. But he felt really proud of the way he'd bounced back today He'd pulled off the kind of thing Freddie was used to doing. He'd taken his chance and grabbed that envelope from Jasper, and he'd looked Finnegan in the eye – and survived. Connor felt good.

He couldn't wait to meet up again tomorrow. *Freddie's really amazing*, he thought, *to have helped all those people alongside Mingoe and Jack.* He wished Freddie's minders from the 17th century could shoot through the vortex and walk protectively either side of him now. That would give Jasper something to think about.

Chapter 11

They met at Freddie's the next morning. Uncle Patrick had taken Kathleen Christmas shopping whilst Finnegan had the dressing changed on a cut over his right eye. He'd tripped over while going to the toilet a couple of nights ago.

Safely in his bedroom, Connor and Ruby pestered Freddie to carry on with his tale. Smiling, he said, "Now here's the good bit, are you ready?"

"We carried on helping plague victims, even when the sights and smells got too much. We only had to think about Sir Bradley and his girls to know we were doing the right thing. We had to keep going. So many people depended on us.

"We changed our protective clothes every three days, replaced the vinegar in the bowl every morning, and soaked our boots in diluted antiseptic every night. We were very careful. We knew one false move could be fatal.

Occasionally, in the middle of all the horror, Freddie saw a collection of survivors walking in groups. They always dressed in white robes, carried long white sticks, and rang handbells, chanting thanks at being saved. They had all shown plague symptoms but somehow survived. "A miracle," Boggy said. "As ninety-nine times out of a hundred it's deadly."

As the Angels approached the dwindling market in Lombard Street one day, a group of thirty or so passed, loudly celebrating their survival. Freddie had to pinch himself. At the front of the column two small boys sang out with rasping voices. Under his adopted white robe, it was easy to see an orange smock top. Striking green eyes shone bright in the strong sunlight and were once again full of life. Freddie was amazed. There were at least two people whose lives they'd affected in a positive way.

And one day it all changed.

Having just stocked their carts with the help of Billy Jenks, they turned into Sweeting's Alley next to the Royal Exchange, only to find their way barricaded by several men. The boys turned to leave, only to find their path back blocked by another group of thugs. Bob Packer stepped menacingly into a shaft of light and the boys clustered together, abandoning their carts. In the background a frail, shrouded figure relayed quiet instructions.

"This 'ere wisp of a man says to take yer carts and yer money, so's you can't look after the plaguers no more. Now, *he* pays me to follow his orders, so I'm telling you to hand it over. All your stock, and every last penny piece. You won't be needing nothin' like that where *you're* going." His men laughed as two thugs approached from behind and two in front, with weapons drawn.

All of a sudden Mingoe and Jack pulled off their hoods and sprang into their well-practised war dance. The men stopped dead in their tracks, unsure of what to do. Packer shouted, "Sort it out. They're just boys. Take 'em, you dogs!" But as they inched forward again, Mingoe and Jack cast pretend spells and gesticulated with such conviction and in such a strange language, that the men faltered for a second time. It was working. Both the shrouded man and Bob were infuriated. Packer shouted, "Fetch me their purses. Now!" The second wave inched forward but halted as they reached their colleagues, who flinched in terror every time one of the boys pointed towards them. How long could they keep this up?

Freddie was desperate to help. He looked around and saw a pyramid of loose cobbles waiting to repair a hole in the alley floor. He picked up several, and without thinking, he started throwing them at the large targets in front and behind. One missed Bob by a whisper as he ducked, but it caught the mysterious figure in the background a glancing blow on his cloaked head. Mingoe and Jack joined Freddie. The three boys pelted their enemies with a ferocious, unrelenting torrent of sharp granite. As the thugs bent over to avoid the barrage, they made easy pickings. Packer was furious with his faltering thugs and urged them on, clearly unwilling to join the assault himself.

"Sort them out!"

Suddenly a piercing cry sounded from the Cornhill end of Sweeting's Alley. Everyone turned to see what it was. They were met with the glorious sight of Billy Jenks leading fifty or so sprinting market stallholders, armed with cudgels, spears and metal bars as weapons. Reinforcements had arrived in the nick of time. Freddie even managed a smile amongst the mayhem.

The arriving army completely scattered the already dazed and confused thugs, chasing them away towards Cornhill or in the other direction to Threadneedle Street, where groups split and separate pursuits continued.

Gasping for breath, with their backs to each other and cobbles ready loaded in hand, the trio looked about them, surveying the battleground. They were alone in the alley and the sounds of the market army dwindled into the distance, but there was no sign of Packer or his injured, hooded paymaster.

They salvaged their carts, two of which had been overturned in the melee. The boys looked at each other.

"I think this will be our last mission," Freddie said. "It's too dangerous. Just because we won today doesn't mean we will tomorrow or next week. We can't walk round with twenty armed guards. They'll get us in the end."

Mingoe and Jack both agreed. They had done well to keep going all this time, and they'd inspired others to help. The churches and the authorities would have to take it from here. "We should concentrate on exposing and ending the Packers for good," said Mingoe. "That's the most important thing we can do."

From high above on a balcony jutting out of the side of the Exchange building, a woman's rough nasal voice stopped them in their tracks.

"End the Packers? You'll be lucky."

The large figure of Old Ma Packer emerged from the shadows.

"Well, well, well. Right nuisance you lot are. You've upset me and my fam'ly." She leaned on the balcony and put the pipe back in her mouth for a good long puff. She seemed in no rush. She had their full attention. "Our friend here wants rid of you three." She gestured with her pipe to someone unseen behind her. He says he'll give us a nice fat load of London sparkle to do that little job for him. I like a bit of sparkle. Don't mind where it comes from. So what are you chicks going to give Ol' Ma to make me forget his offer? Can you boys think of anything I'd like?"

The Angels were silent. Freddie's mind raced and he looked at his comrades. They all knew they could just stroll out of the alley and get away this time, but some bigger battle was being fought here, and they had to find out what it was.

Freddie stalled for time. "We're just trying to help people. We're just trying to make their last days a bit more—"

"I know what you're doing all right, you scrawny whelp! You're stopping my fam'ly doing the same thing. Jus' we charge much higher prices!" She laughed, and two others joined her from the balcony recess. "And anyone who gets in the way of my fam'ly has to deal with me, d'ya understand?"

"You don't frighten us," Freddie blurted. He felt Mingoe and Jack bristle, as if they didn't wholeheartedly agree with his assessment.

"Oh! Well then," she said, tapping out her pipe, "if you're not scared of me, looks like I'll have to lay my Ace card down." She motioned behind her. Bob came to the balcony edge, dragging something, which he heaved above his head and dangled on a rope over the drop.

It was Billy Jenks.

He was gagged and tied securely around his waist

with a thick strap. He desperately tried to wriggle free. Old Ma gestured again to her son, who roughly shook Billy, and the boy's feverish dance of panic subsided as he realised it was futile. His plaintive eyes sought Freddie's for help. It looked like the Packers had found their next 'roper'.

Bob chuckled and nodded at Billy. "I sent his pa to the Indies on a Navy ship. Not that he wanted to go. Got a guinea for him n'all. But, this one, he's worth a lot more."

Old Ma took over. "There's a gentleman here who wants something from your dandy master, that useless excuse, Pepys! And he's going to get it, ain't he! Today! And if it's delivered nice to us, all in one piece, then we'll swap the boy. That's the deal. Take it or leave it. But if you leave it, well, this little chick will be put to work, and he'll last about three days I reckon. That's the average. He won't be a pretty little chick anymore, all plagued up on the end of a rope!"

The hooded figure stepped to the balcony edge and dropped a piece of paper over the side. It turned in the air and landed a few feet away. The boys didn't move, still staring at the swinging lanthorn boy.

"I'd read it if I were you. And I'd do *as* it says, *when* it says, or your little friend here will be a dead chick. Bob hauled on the rope. The ransomed boy jerked upwards towards his grappling arms and the occupants of the balcony disappeared.

The Angels of Mercy were alone. Freddie wondered if they could round up some of the market army to rescue Billy, but they were still scattered, chasing after the gang. The Exchange and its shops were deserted, as they had been for weeks, so Bob and Old Ma could be hiding anywhere. It was hopeless. They had no chance of getting Billy back at the moment. Freddie shook his head in disbelief, trying to fathom what had just happened.

Eventually he made a move towards the folded paper. He read it and offered it to Mingoe and Jack.

"We can't read, Freddie. What do they want?" asked Mingoe.

"Oh, not much." Freddie almost laughed. *Almost.* "They just want some diaries, some cheese... *And me!*"

He looked back down at the spidery writing, calling him to St Paul's at dusk. Then as the first drops of afternoon rain began to fall, the words smudged, and then the distinctive turquoise ink bled and trickled all over the paper until the demands disappeared.

Chapter 12

Freddie prepared for his rendezvous, filling his rucksack, and making a plan for the scenarios that might occur. All of them ended badly.

Pepys was playing the violin in the dining room and intercepted Freddie on his way out.

"Take these precious pages to Cade's of Cornhill. Ask for William Richardson. He alone is to be trusted with them. Tell him to bind them tight. The same size, cover, and spine. And, Fred, these are precious things. I entrust them to you. Now be off."

"Yes, sir," replied Freddie. This complicated things slightly, but gave him a new plan. He scoured Pepys's shelves and got three of the dustiest, most unread books he could find.

The boys had arranged to donate two of their carts to Reverend Vincent who had started similar work, and

Mingoe had taken the Emporium key back to Boggy, and told him about the battle of Sweeting's Alley and the hostage swap at dusk.

"He's mighty fearful for you, Freddie, and wishes you well. Though, he said something strange as I left: 'Watch for the Dark Rider.' I asked him what he meant, but he just smiled and closed his door."

The three boys looked at each other, equally puzzled. Freddie shook his head, "There's no time to work out riddles. There's too much at stake. Saving Billy is the most important thing."

"And you," said Jack quickly.

"Thank you, but let's concentrate on Billy. Whatever happens, I'll be all right." They both nodded reluctantly. "Did you tell the Watch? Are they coming?"

Jack let out a frustrated sigh. "I don't think so. I asked. I even pleaded. I know they believed me, but when I said it was the Packers they lost all interest. Just like that!" He snapped his fingers. "They're too scared. It's up to us I'm afraid."

Retrieving their carts from Whittington Palace, and making their way to Cornhill, Freddie concealed his rucksack under his huge coat. The next hiccup was that John Cade's shop was closed. Freddie tried knocking on the door and shouting up at the windows, but there was no answer. He couldn't believe it. He was guarding the third volume of Pepys's diaries and about to face the Packers. He knew the diaries were what the shrouded figure wanted, and had hoped they'd be safely locked up in Cade's shop by now. If he had to swap the pages for Billy then he would, but he'd do all he could to save both.

They donated two of their carts to the Reverend Vincent, as planned, but before they left the privacy of his yard in Milk Street, Jack curled up on the third, and along with two 'borrowed' cutlasses from Sir William Batten's collection, he was hidden under a metre-sized round board, like a shield, which he held in place with a large strap attached to the underside. Then the canvas was draped over it. He was about the size of a curled-up Great Dane and perfectly disguised as Pepys's favourite cheese: a 40-kilogram round of Parmesan, all the way from Italy, and worth its weight in gold.

"Are you comfortable?" asked Mingoe with a smile.

"What do you think?" replied Jack, shifting his weight. "Drive slowly over the cobbles."

What a risk they were taking! Three boys, two cutlasses and one wooden shield, against the might of the Packers. But Jack was their surprise. The plan had to work.

Constant bells sounded around them, mourning the dead. They walked against a tide of corpses being transported to mass graves beyond the city walls.

"Let's split up. I'm meant to be alone. I'll go round the south side of St Paul's and you creep down from the north. Good luck."

Mingoe nodded. "I'm ready, and, Jack, remember the cue is—"

"I know the cue! Just make sure I can hear it."

He passed one of the razor-sharp cutlasses from under the canvas.

"For Billy, and Sir Bradley. For them all!" said Freddie quietly.

"For them all," the three whispered intently.

"Quickly, before the light fades." But Mingoe was already gone. Freddie rattled the cart on, past the closed booksellers' cabins. The plan was to ensure Mingoe spirited Billy away, whilst Jack surprised the gang and divided their ranks. Freddie would draw attention away from the rescue and when Billy, Mingoe and Jack were safe he would recite 'If—' and escape through the vortex. Simple!

The mighty cathedral bell rang seven. It would be dark within the hour. Freddie positioned the cart on the corner exactly where the portal would open. He whispered, "Good luck," to Jack and looked around, studying the shadows, searching for shapes. He couldn't see anyone, but that didn't mean he wasn't being watched.

He climbed high up the scaffolding to survey his troops on the battlefield. Except he only had *two* troops, and one of those was pretending to be a cheese!

Freddie made use of the time by gathering up potential missiles. As the remaining members of the gang emerged into the square, several hobbled and sported bandages or slings. "Good," he whispered.

But then, up the stairs from the crypt came half a dozen fit men, and from the surrounding alleys and lanes, boys emerged, obviously having checked nearby for any hidden reinforcements. They took up positions around the perimeter amongst more thugs, who emerged from the shadows.

Would the Watch turn up? Freddie wondered.

He caught sight of Mingoe directly behind three of the perimeter thugs. It was a perfect position. Tension was mounting in the gloom.

Then came more movement from Ludgate. The shrouded figure was leading Billy on a rope. He dragged and pulled his blindfolded captive, but the old man was tiring, constantly battling with the boy.

"Stop pulling, or your end will come sooner than you expect," his thin voice echoed. Billy didn't struggle any more, but simply lay down on the ground so he had to be dragged. One of the thugs helped and they eventually pulled Billy to a stop by the cathedral steps.

Freddie scanned the scene. It felt like the curtain call at a play with everyone waiting for the main actors to enter for their applause. He didn't have long to wait.

From the north side, and passing close by to Mingoe, came Aggie brandishing her glinting knife. Behind her, Bob strode confidently with a cudgel resting on his shoulder. And finally Old Ma Packer processed into the arena drawing on her pipe and surveying the layout of her troops.

They stopped on the cathedral steps, a few metres from Billy. Bob turned on the spot as he spoke. "Come on then, Irish. Show yerself. Ma wants her supper, we ain't got all night."

Old Ma Packer removed her pipe and spat on the ground at Billy's feet. Bob continued, "I'll count to ten, and if you don't appear… Billy boy here gets a knock on the head, with this." He brandished the cudgel. "And then tomorrow he starts his new line of work – still on the rope, but *this* time, he'll be in and out of houses."

The shrouded man paced impatiently, looking everywhere for Freddie. He neared the cart, obviously about to inspect the cheese. Freddie had to intervene. The moment had come!

"Here I am." Everyone peered up until they could pick out Freddie. He stood defiantly and shed his black cloak.

"So, there you are, Irish. Not such a clever place to hide, is it? My boys will be up there in a second. By the time I count to ten you…"

"I wouldn't overwork your feeble brain counting past three, Bob Packer, I doubt if you can anyway," Freddie yelled, and then, hoping Jack could hear, he shouted, "*FOR BILLY, FOR SIR BRADLEY. FOR THEM ALL!*"

On which cue, Mingoe attacked the three nearest cutthroats, and Jack rose like a ghost using the wooden circle as a shield, swirling about on top of the cart. He sliced the attacking weapons of the surprised gang with his flashing cutlass.

The shrouded man stood beneath Freddie, shouting up at him.

"Give me what's mine, you—" Freddie pelted him with his collection of tools, tiles and small stone pieces, scattering the gang. He managed to hit several of them, but it was the chaos he created that was the most valuable element. The surprise had worked, but soon the tables would turn.

Then all at once carts, carriages, and a mob of screaming market traders, led by a masked figure on a black horse stampeded into Cathedral Square from all directions. They made short work of the scattering gang members who were easily picked off and overpowered.

The Dark Rider charged straight for Bob Packer as he raised his cudgel to strike Billy. The horseman kicked the thug to the ground, and hauled Billy onto his saddle where the boy scrabbled to untie his blindfold. They made straight for the cluster still fighting around Mingoe and the horse soon scared them off into the waiting arms of the butchers, brewers and bakers who, for the second time today, cheered the capture of each villainous racketeer.

Bob limped away with help, and the two women had disappeared. The battle was won. But Jack was hurt. Freddie had seen him caught by a blow from a cudgel, and now he was lying unprotected in a daze on top of the cart.

The shrouded man reacted quickest, and dragged Jack onto the ground by his metal collar. Brandishing a small knife at his throat, he backed towards the scaffolding and shouted, "Leave me alone or this boy will breathe his last." The mob was unsure what to do. The Dark Rider and Mingoe joined them, surrounding the loathsome man.

Freddie knew he was positioned perfectly. He had to recite his homeward mantra, jump from the scaffolding, knock the shrouded man away from Jack and then enter the vortex. Simple – *Not!*

"If you can keep your head…" He spoke as fast as he could.

Down below, people were testing the knife-wielding man. As a few dashed in from one side, he made to cut Jack's neck.

The Dark Rider called, "Stop! Let's be calm about this."

That sounds like Boggy, Freddie thought, whilst all the time reciting at speed, "If you can make one heap of all your winnings—Aaarrrgh." A huge hand grabbed his throat from behind. Bob Packer had climbed the scaffolding and now he had hold of Freddie. His heart pounded as he dangled over the edge.

"You'd better let that gentleman go," Bob shouted down to the crowd. They gasped in horror as they looked up and saw what was unfolding. "Now back off, away from him, quick now. Or this will be the end of Irish."

The crowd slowly stepped back. Freddie had automatically carried on reciting 'If—', hoping the portal would understand and appear. 'If you can talk with crowds and keep your virtue...' sounded like a series of gurgles. Freddie was about to give up hope when a shimmering mauve light began pulsing at the foot of the scaffolding.

The shrouded figure, pointing at Freddie, screamed, "No! Stop him! Stop his words!" He definitely sounded upset.

"Stop what?" called Bob. "He's not talking, he's gasping for air." Mingoe used the distraction and dashed forward, knocking the knife away from Jack's throat. He punched the shrouded figure so hard the man fell on the ground right by the portal opening. Then Mingoe dragged Jack to safety.

Freddie reached the end, "And—which is more—you'll be a Man, my son!" He kicked himself forward and toppled over the edge of the scaffolding. Leaving Packer empty-handed, Freddie dropped like a stone and thudded feet first into the back of the shrouded figure, who was attempting to stand. The two of them shot through the portal and hurtled along the vortex in the ferocious torrent of wind that sped them away from 1665. Freddie felt like he was only semi-conscious. He could see the shrouded figure tumbling ahead of him, but lost sight of his enemy on a bend in the tunnel.

"The next thing I remember is waking up on the floor of my bedroom with a massive headache, sore all over. The map was whole again and I was home. I didn't want to move but I struggled out of my rucksack and opened the zip. *What was I going to do?* I'd returned with a whole chunk of Pepys's famous diary and..."

Freddie closed his eyes and shook his head. "You'll never guess what else. It was just staring at me, with its head peeping out of the rucksack..."

"Freddie. Tell us."

"A rat! A massive black rat!"

Ruby gaped at him in horror.

"WHAT?"

Chapter 13

"You are joking, aren't you?" Ruby started smiling.

"C'mon, Freddie. Don't mess with us," pleaded Connor.

Moments later they stood in the shed at the bottom of Freddie's garden looking at the twitching whiskers of a large black rat.

"Samuel," said Freddie. "I've called him Samuel after…"

Ruby shook her head and stared at Samuel with wide eyes. "But what if he's got fleas!? What if he's brought the plague?"

"That's why I need you guys to help with a plan. I've got him in this plastic box with air holes. What else can I do?"

"Well, if you keep him warm and fed, if he does have fleas they'll stay on him. They'd only want to leave the rat, err... *Samuel*, if Samuel dies. Why would they want to move otherwise?" reasoned Connor.

"Brilliant, Conman. Absolute top thinking. So basically we've got to keep Samuel alive," said Ruby.

Freddie continued, "No one ever comes in here, so I'll just nip in once a day and feed him 'til we come up with a permanent solution."

"You've got to make sure no one sees you," said Connor.

"I'll do it," Ruby offered. "I can go through the hole in the hedge."

Freddie nodded.

"All right, if you're sure. Best after dark though."

"No probs, buddy. So let's see this diary then. It'd better be good!"

Back in Freddie's room they surveyed the sheets, about the size of a really thick school exercise book. There was the date at the top of the first page and then just random squiggles and numbers, with only the occasional full words like Creed, White Hall or Batten.

"Wow!" said Connor, stretching a finger out. Then, remembering some of his past mistakes with valuable treasures, he retracted it and smiled sheepishly. "What does it say?"

Freddie stared and concentrated for a moment.

"'Wednesday 1st July 1663. This morning it rained so hard, though it was fair yesterday...' And on it goes. He likes talking about rain."

"I hope it's not all about the weather," Ruby interrupted. "How are we going to get it back?"

As if in sympathy with the trio, the map sprang to life. All the characters started thinking. Atlas put down his globe, sat on it and scratched his head. The Yeti and Tutankhamun were in animated conversation, and the Druid was pleading to the sky. Suddenly, the characters fled as hundreds of tiny rats appeared from nowhere, swarming around the globe, making Ruby, Connor and Freddie escape his bedroom and stand bewildered on the landing.

They needed to find out more about the diaries, and the library was warm and rodent free, an inviting escape from the winter chill outside.

"This says, 'In September at least 30,000 people died, and 100,000 died altogether. London only had a population of 500,000 before the plague, so the disease killed one in five of the population!'... That's incredible!" gasped Ruby.

"This book says it was predicted, because a comet was seen in the sky in 1664, and everyone knew something bad was going to happen," Connor added.

And something bad did then happen. Casey,

Anna and Nell shuffled in. They were dressed in their trademark tracksuits and baseball caps. Connor thought they looked like joke gangsters. But he wished he wasn't still scared of them. Even Ruby looked tense. She was like a cat ready to spring into action should anything start.

Casey spied Connor, then sat by the radiator and started texting. Pushing some books towards the boys, Ruby said, "You guys put these back. And then make it look like you're looking for some other stuff by the fire escape. And then when Casey's not looking, get out of here! I'll check they don't follow you. See you back at Freddie's when the coast's clear... I'll be fine." Her look at Connor stopped his protest. "They don't care about me, they don't even know we're friends."

"Yes they do. They see us at school all the time."

"Yeah! All right, they do. But they wouldn't dare take me on." Ruby arched her eyebrows.

Freddie and Connor nodded. She had a point. Ruby was stronger, fitter, fiercer, cleverer and *always*, absolutely right.

"OK, but text us. Follow as soon as you can."

Ruby smiled and patted Connor's arm. "I'll be fine. Get going!"

The boys sauntered over to put their books away. Freddie sussed out the fire exit as Connor pretended to study the nearby shelves before he realised he was looking intently at the 'Expectant Parent' section. He heard the door click open and Freddie hiss, "Now."

A second later they were outside, but froze as Jasper, Kelvin and Maz crossed the end of the alley, obviously on their way in through the main library doors. Connor's heart hammered away as Freddie blew out a stream of air.

"That was close, but Casey will tell them. Let's run."

Connor didn't hesitate.

As they raced away across the market square to lose themselves in the streets opposite, he managed to send a text to Ruby.

JASPER!

YEP! HE'S HERE

And that was the last they heard from Ruby for over 350 years.

Freddie and Connor kept glancing over their shoulders as they dashed to safety. They turned and waited. "I can't see her," said Freddie.

"We shouldn't have left her," wheezed Connor, his face crimson with the cold and the effort.

When they were safe in Freddie's bedroom with the last slabs of lemon drizzle cake from the kitchen table, Freddie tried to call Ruby for the third time and sent yet another text.

"No answer!"

Every time they failed to make contact with her, Connor felt his gut twist with worry. The map was in chaos. It felt like a new adventure might not be far off. They checked their rucksacks and waited for the map to whisk them away.

Freddie frowned. "What if I'm not here for tea? My parents will go crazy. They'll break the door down and see I've gone through the wall."

"No they won't," Connor told him. "It closes when you're away. Remember? I got stuck in it when you went back to Nepal."

"Oh, yes," said Freddie, smiling. "But I hope we're not away for long."

It got dark, and Ruby didn't phone or text back. Connor watched the time go by on Freddie's alarm clock and started to feel a bit ill. After the fifth voicemail and tenth text, Freddie gave up. "It's no good, we've got to find out what's happened. She could be in all sorts of trouble. Where shall we start?"

But they were too late. From the hall downstairs came the sound of Finnegan and Kathleen demanding tea and cake. It stopped the boys in their tracks. Connor didn't want to risk an encounter with the hateful old man and another barrage of personal insults. One look at Freddie told him his friend was thinking the same.

"Let's climb out of the window, down into the garden, and get away," said Freddie, undoing the latch and lifting it open, ready to scramble out.

Connor backed away and shook his head. "I can't climb down, Freddie. Finnegan will go into the lounge in a bit, then…"

Freddie dropped the window down. "OK, but let's be ready."

But Finnegan didn't go into the lounge. Instead, he very loudly climbed the stairs. "Well I want lemon drizzle cake. It was there this morning." He slammed the toilet door near Freddie's bedroom. They were trapped until he went back downstairs.

"Urgh! It's not even his house," Freddie said.

A rumbling sound started up from behind the map. The scattered characters raced back to their homelands and the rats converged on London. The last one looked around, sniffed, and followed its friends down a large hole.

Hymns, then guitars and drums were drowned out by bagpipes and trumpets. Plane engines roared around the room, pickaxes on stone, radio news and adverts. Neptune yawned and stretched. He puffed his cheeks, before winking at the boys and blowing his familiar tornado. They grabbed their rucksacks and sat back down on the bed. The loose pages of Pepys's diary began fluttering. Freddie dived on the pile and got them safely into his rucksack and out of danger. The usual jumble of loose clothes circled above their heads in the maelstrom, and Connor was knocked on the forehead by his own recorder, which he'd purposely left in Mr M's car after the school play, hoping never to see it again. He grabbed it on its next circuit and stuffed it deep in his bag by a pack of biscuits.

What would they tell Ruby? Where was she?

A tear appeared in the map. "Here we go!" shouted Freddie. Connor held his breath and closed his eyes as the chaos in the room intensified. Freddie shot towards the wall as if pulled by a giant bungee rope. A second later, it was Connor's turn. Freddie surged through the gap with Connor following, catching the sides painfully with his elbows. They were off!

Screaming with both the thrill of the launch and the pain from his arms, Connor caught Freddie and they managed to stabilise their flight and stop each other bumping into the spongy vortex walls.

Connor was enthralled by the portals along the way. First, the vista of deep space, then the World War I trench, and a new portal where a gladiator faced a lion. He was pleased they weren't stopping at any of those.

Finally they were slowed by a strong headwind and helpful spirits began fussing around them supportively.

Connor knew they had reached the right portal, but it was clearly night-time on the other side and impossible to pick out any clues or landmarks. As the wind subsided they looked at one another and stepped through the screen, but the flashing lights of the vortex made it difficult to adjust to the sudden darkness.

"Quick, what's the date?" asked Freddie. Both boys spun round to see the numbers floating away.

"Did you see?" Freddie whispered into the dark.

"No, but there were a lot of sixes flying about."

"Where's your torch?"

The first thing they saw when Freddie shone the beam was the wooden scaffolding and painted sign listing services for St Paul's.

"Oh! Wow! Connor, we're back, we're in London again."

Connor couldn't believe it. *So far so good*, he thought. "But when? How will we find out?"

"We'll just have to ask somebody, I guess." With that, he and Connor set off in the direction of Pepys's home.

"Be very careful where you walk and what you touch. If the plague is still here just copy what I do, OK?"

Connor nodded, looking understandably worried.

"Right. But not too fast please, Freddie," he said. "These cobbles are really weird to walk on.

"All right, mate, just stick with me. I've got an idea

of how we find out the date."

They stood by the side door of Garraway's coffeehouse, rifling through the old unwanted news sheets.

"Did you know there are over eighty coffee houses around Cornhill and the Exchange," Connor said, sounding like an encyclopaedic sat nav. Freddie turned.

"How do you know that?"

"I read it in the library. Hang on, what's this? 1666. This one says, *Oxford Gazette*, 18th of August, this one says the 25th."

"So it's 1666," said Freddie, with a huge sigh of relief. "Thank goodness for that, we're in the clear. The plague will be over. At least I hope so."

Chapter 14

Meanwhile in the library, over 350 years later, Ruby packed her things away, never taking her eyes off the collection of tracksuits gathering by the photocopier. She was confident that the boys had got away. Now she had to do the same.

She casually gathered the remaining books in front of her as a librarian told the gang to move away from the machine. It was a helpful diversion, and she quickly made for the fire exit, as Maz and Rowan left via the main door. She deposited the plague books amongst the Babycare section and slipped out of the fire escape, just metres ahead of Maz and Rowan who were running down the alley towards her. Ruby sprinted off, knowing she would be too quick for them. Behind her the fire exit banged open, unleashing Jasper and Kelvin to join the chase.

This was a new one for Ruby. She was half petrified at being pursued by the gang of bullies and half exhilarated at the idea she could easily outwit them. She crossed to the other side of the Market Square and hid behind a post van. The boys stood in the middle of the space, dumbfounded. They were joined by Anna, Nell and Casey, who triumphantly handed something to Jasper.

It was a phone.

Ruby's hand went to her pocket where she knew hers was. Except it wasn't! She panicked and searched all her layers. Nothing. She rifled through the carrier bag. Nothing! Then she remembered. She'd been researching Pepys on her phone whilst Connor was using the book she needed.

"No!" she cried. She'd left her phone in the rush and Casey must have taken it. How could she have made such a stupid mistake?

Her mind raced, trying to calculate the danger of her phone in their hands. It was locked and they wouldn't be able to open it without her passcode. Good. And even if they did, there was nothing on it about the map, Egypt, or the vortex; she'd always made sure of that. The main problems as far as she could see were that her mum would be furious, and she couldn't get hold of Freddie and Connor. She decided to race to Normandy Avenue as soon as possible to stop everyone worrying.

The post van was ready to drive off. The gang looked like they were heading straight for Normandy Avenue too, maybe thinking they could catch Connor and Freddie. Ruby's brain raced with possibilities and outcomes. She could buy her friends some time. *What if I let them see me? Then lead them all over the place and put them off the scent.* It was a brave plan. "Let's give it a go," she said.

Jasper and the other tracksuits were still fifty metres away when Ruby stepped out in front of them. They stopped and looked at each other. This was obviously not what they were expecting. Jasper lifted the phone and waved it at Ruby. She shrugged and turned away from Normandy Avenue. They took the bait. At a gentle jog, she led them all around the streets.

One by one her pursuers dropped out, she guessed either too tired or bored. She darted down turnings, then surged on again. In the end just the wheezing Kelvin and the super-fit Jasper still followed. But Ruby always had just enough stamina to keep ahead. She was enjoying this. She imagined telling the boys her tale, and their eyes wide with admiration.

It was about half an hour before Jasper and Kelvin gave up. Ruby had run them in a circle and taken them back to the library. Under the white light of a streetlamp she saw Jasper hold up the phone, smile, and drop it on the ground. Then both he and Kelvin stamped on it several times before casually walking away.

Once she was sure they were gone, she quickly retrieved the SIM card from the shattered phone. At least she had that.

Feeling proud of her amazing self-preservation skills, she made straight for Freddie's house. She felt alive, powerful and clever. *Actually, anyone was clever compared to Jasper and Kelvin*, she thought.

Turning the corner into Normandy Avenue, she saw Uncle Patrick slowly unloading Finnegan and Kathleen from his car and shepherding them like angry geese up the path. How could she get past them and up to Freddie's room? Simple. The back garden, then up onto the flat roof, knock on the window and, '*Surprise!*' Yes!

First, she checked all was OK at home, then having grabbed a pack of ginger nuts, she went out into the dark garden and through the hedge to Freddie's house. She'd think of an excuse to tell her mum about the broken phone later. Freddie's bedroom light was on. Good. She quickly dropped four biscuits in with Samuel and closed the shed door.

As she looked back up at his bedroom, she saw an amazing sight. Lights from every colour of the spectrum bounced around the walls, and although no sound could be heard, it was obvious what was happening.

Oh, no! Not again! Ruby raced up to the house and scrambled swiftly up onto the flat roof of the extension. She pressed her nose to the window. The map was alive and teeming with movement around the huge hole at its centre. Objects circled the room in a tornado above Freddie's bed. The hole was beginning to close. Ruby pulled up the window and stepped into the frenzy.

The wind nearly knocked her off her feet. She managed to close the window behind her and staggered to the end of the bed. Should she just dive through and hope for the best?

She caught a glimpse of the shrouded figure beyond the map in the vortex. He turned, saw her and pushed at the edges, trying to close the gap from the other side.

I'm going to sort that guy out. She struggled towards the map, but it took all her might to move her feet. The hole was closing fast. Time was running out. Sensing victory, the hooded figure waved at her and shrieked a triumphant cackle. All of a sudden Atlas ran from the west of the map, quadrupling his size as he threw himself into the hole, using his back, arms and legs to stop it closing. He turned and nodded at Ruby.

The Yeti, Tutankhamun and Druid all shot out hands to drag her through, and with everyone's combined strength she scrambled into the vortex, and was whisked away along the tunnel. Atlas waved and the map closed behind her.

She was on her way. *This is insane!* she thought as she surged into the jet stream.

At the same time as marvelling at the vortex and its hundreds of possibilities, Ruby was running through a mental checklist. She disappeared through the map at about 5 pm on December 23rd. She hoped wherever she went it was a quick visit, as she didn't want to miss Christmas. So if Freddie was away for four months in London time, but less than five hours in real time, she needed to enter the right portal, find the boys, and persuade them to return immediately, so her mum wouldn't worry.

She spied the shrouded figure ahead clinging to the vortex wall, away from the ferocious air currents, lying in wait for her. Ruby realised her best weapon was her winter boots. She turned in the slipstream, now travelling feet first. As the shrouded figure made a grab, she kicked out at his stomach on the way past.

On she surged, spinning away from the sinister figure. The headwind in front increased to slow her down and the familiar friendly spirits that she remembered from the journey to Egypt circled and fluttered around. She grabbed the frame of the inky black portal, hoping desperately it was the same entrance Freddie and Connor had just used. *How would she find them?*

The figures pointed and urged her through, nodding as she put a foot towards the plasma screen. Taking a deep breath as if diving underwater, she plunged through. Ruby turned to see the portal's outline fade and the friendly spirits disappear.

"1666! Ooops," she said, as the time code floated away, and she wondered if the boys had gone back to 1665. How would she find out? Thoughts zapped about her brain. 'Clothes', 'Maps', 'Rucksa…' "Oh! No!" she blurted. She'd forgotten to get her rucksack.

"Calm down, Ruby," she said out loud. She reasoned that she knew where the portal was, and she had learned 'If—', their homeward mantra, so if all else failed she could get back here and return home.

Ruby was nevertheless excited. She felt strong and capable, but a huge part of her wished Freddie and Connor were at her side. She thought of all the things Freddie had said: The first few minutes are the most important; You have to get to safety; Take in as much information as you can.

She turned slowly on the spot, observing her surroundings. Then she saw the wooden sign for St Paul's that Freddie had talked about. Her shoulders relaxed and she breathed a huge sigh of relief – until she remembered the plague!

Realising she was right by the headquarters of the Packer gang, she moved quickly away and used Freddie's descriptions to head in the direction of Cheapside, a reverse of the last journey Freddie had taken with the fake cheese. Ruby was pleased with herself for listening so carefully to Freddie's adventure. All that information was flooding back as she picked up the pace. But she needed some different clothes from somewhere.

High on the wooden scaffolding, a small boy in an orange smock top scampered along, charting Ruby's progress, before soundlessly dropping down to the ground and descending the steps to the crypt.

At the same time the purple outline of the portal shimmered, and a bent shape gingerly stepped through the plasma screen. Still holding his stomach from Ruby's powerful kick, the shrouded figure emerged and shakily leaned against the cathedral wall. He watched the blue-haired girl walk away, and a cruel smile danced on his pained lips.

Chapter 15

Pepys flicked excitedly through the lost pages. "Thank God they're safe, and that *you* are, Fred, and your companion."

"Connor, sir," said Freddie.

"Oh! Another Irishman?"

"Well, not exactly, sir, but my best friend."

"Well, that's good. Tell me how you've come to be absent for a year all the while in possession of these important papers."

Freddie had to think quickly.

"Well if you remember, a year ago I took them for binding, but the shop was closed due to plague, and... On the way back, I was attacked by a gang who kidnapped me and... And forced me onto a ship. I told them I was your servant, but they didn't believe me. But as I could read and write I had to serve the captain as his cabin boy, and the next morning we sailed for Barbados. It took weeks to cross the ocean, and after we docked, from deep in the ship 200 slaves were led up in chains to stand on the quayside. The captain was given bags of gold and we loaded up with sugar. That is, after the hold was emptied of the slaves who had died on the voyage.

"They were thrown over the side of the ship and left to float away. 'Food for the fishes', the captain said.

"For months we traded around the islands and the captain grew richer, and the crew more desperate for his gold. Eventually they mutinied and threw the captain overboard. 'Food for the fishes', said the ringleader to the crew, and they turned the ship around and with a cargo of molasses we sailed back here."

Pepys sat open mouthed, unable to quite fathom the story.

"And... Connor?" he asked, bemused.

"Ah! Yes, sir, Connor... Our assistant cook, and a wonderful ally. He helped me keep your papers safe when the crew threatened to burn them. He hid them under his shirt, that's how they survived." Freddie looked at Connor, whose initial expression of bewilderment changed to a smile of admiration at his friend's quick thinking.

"Yes, sir," he agreed, nodding vigorously. Connor stood in a brown shirt like Freddie's and an old pair of servant's breeches that appeared severely stretched.

It all itched, and he kept scratching his neckline where the material rubbed. The pair fell silent, waiting for Pepys's reaction.

"Well I never! And the ship's name?"

"The *Hispaniola*, sir," said Freddie.

"Captain?"

"Flint, sir," he stuttered in reply.

"And leader of the mutiny?"

"Long John Silver, sir," Connor confidently took over, having suddenly realised that Freddie was using *Treasure Island* characters to fill out his invented plot.

"I've never heard of the *Hispaniola*. Where is she now?"

"Unloaded, sir, and the crew sold it to… err, Squire Trelawney. It sailed at first light this morning." Freddie finished with a flourish, thoroughly pleased with himself.

"Well, well. What an adventure you've had! I'm glad you're both safe and my papers are returned. So I s'pose you want your old job back, unless that is, you got a share of the ship's bounty?"

"No, sir, we were robbed by three sailors, sir, Gunn, Pugh, and…" Freddie ran out of inspiration.

"Smollett!" Connor helped.

"Thank goodness we've both read the same book," said Freddie minutes later as he showed Connor his old room in the attic.

"How did you invent all that so quickly, about the

slaves and everything."

"I didn't invent that, I really didn't," said Freddie simply. "That part was all true. It's unbelievable. That's what happened to Mingoe's dad on the way from Africa. They were laid out on wooden racks and shackled with chains for weeks on end. Once a day, if they were lucky, they were allowed up on deck for a few moments' exercise and some food. Every day fewer and fewer slaves were fit enough to make it to the fresh air. And every day more and more died and were just left chained in the hold, until they reached the West Indies. Mingoe's dad had to help remove the unlucky ones."

The two boys sat in stunned silence. They thought *they* had problems with the bullying they faced daily at school, but that evaporated into complete insignificance compared to the slave traders' atrocious inhumanity. They struggled to even begin to imagine the horrors the slaves faced, not just on their torturous journey across the Atlantic, but throughout their lives, working only to make their white masters rich beyond imagination.

Connor was to help in Pepys's kitchen assisting the temperamental cook, who spent most of her time drinking and sleeping rather than working. As he watched pots boil and stews simmer, Connor added his own distinctive extra touches, transforming the kitchen produce into very much more palatable offerings.

Whenever possible he practised his recorder, which sounded really good in the echoey kitchen. The tempting smells lured Pepys downstairs where he saw Connor happily creating a lamb stew, whilst playing the theme from the Pied Piper school play. Towards the end he noticed Pepys listening at the open door and he squeaked and squawked as a result. Pepys was impressed nevertheless and said, "Very good, boy. You surprise me. Our food has improved and you delight my ear as well. What else do you play? Violin perhaps?"

"No, nothing else, sir. I have only just started the recorder."

"Recorder, is that what you call it? You must try the flageolet after supper this evening. I am looking for help at my recitals."

"Yes, sir," said Connor, wondering what terrible can of worms he had opened.

And so over three days Connor made himself indispensable in the household, revolutionising the food served, and after supper every night learning and playing music with Pepys and his guests. His travelling superpowers had returned – as he had been in Egypt, he was once more a whizz in the kitchen. The power of the map helping him excel yet again.

Freddie introduced Connor to Mingoe and Jack, who were overjoyed to see Freddie. Both had grown about a foot since the plague days of a year ago. And the growth spurt had only added to Jack's smile and Mingoe's strength. Freddie was incredibly thankful they had survived the pestilence.

They both admitted they assumed him dead or press-ganged, and Freddie repeated a dramatically edited version of *Treasure Island* to convince them about his absence. The diary pages were finally deposited at John Cade's shop for binding, and showing Connor around the plague-free streets, the four boys sat safely in Cornhill watching the world go by.

"Is Billy safe and well?" asked Freddie.

"Yes, he's fine. He works for Boggy, fetching and carrying."

"I bet Boggy was the Dark Rider!" blurted Connor, who blushed instantly. All three looked at him and smiled kindly.

"You're right," said Jack. "We see him a lot. He's been helping us with something," said Jack. He and Mingoe smiled at each other and produced Sir Bradley Roast's letter.

"I'd forgotten all about it," said Freddie.

"So did we. We were so glad to have rescued Billy, and so busy looking for you, that it was at least two months before we remembered and went back for it," said Jack.

"What does it say?"

"We couldn't read it, and we didn't know who to trust," Jack continued, "so we went to see Boggy…"

The boys smiled at each other again and Mingoe handed over the letter.

It was a copy of Sir Bradley's will, signed by him, his five daughters, and a lawyer, Richard Leeming, of Howard, Leeming, Farnsworth and Leech. A lot of official information was followed by,

> Myself and my five daughters, Trinity, Mercy, Charity, Faith and Patience leave all our worldly goods to be divided thus. My London house and half my fortune I leave to my friend, Sir Richard Parsons and his family, of Fleet Street.
>
> My Devon farm and lands, and the other half of my fortune I leave to be divided three ways between Mingoe, [indentured to Sir William Batten] Jack, [indentured to Sir William Penn] and Freddie Malone, [servant and secretary to Samuel Pepys], all of Seething Lane.
>
> Should the pestilence take any or all of the above mentioned, their share should instead go to the surviving beneficiaries. If none are left alive then the monies should go to the upkeep of Grace Church on Grace Church Street.

Then followed all the signatures, dates and witnesses.

Freddie looked up to see Mingoe and Jack smiling, as thrilled again as they must have been when Boggy had first read the will to them. Connor's face was also a picture of wonder, excited about what this meant for the future.

"Amazing! WOW! What are we waiting for?" marvelled Freddie.

"There's one problem," Mingoe began. "We went to their office in Mark Lane and presented ourselves. But Howard, Leeming, and Farnsworth all died from the pestilence, leaving only a man we don't trust, called Abel Leech.

"He tried to keep our copy, Jack had to wrench it out of his hands – can you see that crease and small tear. Then Boggy found out that the other man, Sir Richard Parsons, had also died of the plague, and all his family. Which means, the three of us are set to inherit everything! Then Leech accused us of murdering you, Freddie, in order to inherit your share. He threatened to report us unless we give up our share of the fortune. We tried to find Boggy but he's been away for months. His shop is being run by someone else. We're so scared of doing something wrong and ruining our claim, but now you're back. The miracle is alive once more."

"We will definitely get it sorted out. But what about the indentures to your masters?"

"Boggy told us we can buy them back. We can give back exactly the amount paid for us and be free men. We won't have to wait until we're fifty to start our lives, after all," said Jack, with tears forming in his eyes.

"But we need help, because this man Leech really

lives up to his name. It's too dangerous to ask our masters. But now we can go to Leech and prove you're alive, and become free men. Let's go now!" Mingoe beamed.

The boys walked in a daze towards Leech's office in Mark Lane, one road over from Seething Lane. The houses they passed which had been emptied by the plague were now full again. It was as if it had never happened. People laughed and jostled, spat and shouted, kissed and shook hands. Except for the chiming of the hours, the bells had stopped their constant ringing. London seemed peculiar to Freddie in the fiercely hot late-August sunshine, because it was normal.

Connor took everything in so he could tell Ruby when they got back. He hoped she was all right. He watched Freddie walking between Mingoe and Jack and wondered what would happen with Sir Bradley's will. It all sounded so complicated. All he knew about lawyers was what his dad once said, 'They just serve themselves, make life as complicated as possible, and fleece everyone'.

They can't all be like that, thought Connor, but when they stood opposite Abel Leech's office, it didn't take long to get a bad impression of the man. They saw him strut out of his door like a peacock.

Jack said, "He wears new outfits every day. When we first met him, he was dressed in tattered old clothes. Something's changed." Leech strode down

Mark Lane on his spindly legs, followed by the boys at a discreet distance.

Freddie was rapidly forming his own strong dislike of Leech. He frowned at Mingoe and Jack. "He doesn't look like a man who's upset that his business partners have died of the plague."

Leech turned right onto Thames Street. Freddie frowned.

"Where's he going? Let's split up, two and two. He doesn't know me and Connor, so we can get close so we don't lose him."

Moments later, Leech stopped on the corner of Dice Quay and looked furtively about. Mingoe and Jack were hidden in a doorway, but Freddie and Connor walked on casually. Leech ignored them and turned towards the Packers' warehouse.

Freddie and Connor saw Leech knock on the door and disappear inside. The four boys congregated and decided it was too dangerous to be seen near the Packers' Treasury. Then Freddie had a bright idea.

"Connor! They don't know you. You can watch and then follow Leech back?"

"I've got to be back for my vegetable prep," he said feebly. Freddie could see he was understandably anxious to be left alone in 17th-century London, amongst the most evil men in the city, but he also thought Connor was up to the task. He just needed a little encouragement.

"He's got to come back this way, so you can hide on the corner and watch his movements. I'll do your vegetables for you."

Connor paused for a moment, then nodded.

"All right, but don't forget the salt. And Samuel likes everything in small pieces, so cut them like this." Connor indicated the size. Freddie could see he wasn't comfortable. "What happens if I get caught?"

"You'll be fine. You know your way back. We're going to find out where Boggy's gone. Good luck, mate."

Connor watched them disappear and he took up what he thought looked like a natural position outside the busy Dolphin Tavern. He could just see the warehouse door, but he had to appear occupied. The only thing he could think of doing was to play his recorder which he now had on him at all times at Pepys's insistence. He ran through his repertoire, and the odd coin was thrown at his feet by admiring passers-by. He had no idea how much money he was collecting, but it was proving the perfect cover. Connor's confidence grew.

Freddie, Mingoe and Jack knocked on the locked door of Boggy's shop, and a young man with a bad limp answered, "Yes?"

"We're looking for William Boghurst, sir. Can you help us? We're friends of his," said Freddie.

"He's due back any day. He's been travelling the

Continent finding out how to battle the plague, should it ever return. Try again next week. Who shall I say asked for him?"

"Just say, friends of the Dark Rider, he'll know who we are." They turned to go, but the young man said, "Are you the Angels of Mercy he talks about in his lectures?"

"Yes, sir, we are. Freddie, Jack, and I'm Mingoe."

The man smiled and looked at the boys with deep admiration.

"I've heard all about you. He always mentions you, and says what a debt of gratitude this city owes you. When he returns I will send a message. Where can I find you? We have a boy, Billy Jenks, who runs all our errands."

"We know Billy," said Freddie, smiling broadly with the others. "He knows exactly where to find us. Tell him to run all the way when Boggy returns. Thank you again."

Freddie wore a wide smile as they made their way through the summer streets. Today felt like a preparation day. Setting lots of things in motion, which would all bear fruit later on. *Hopefully.*

Now there were vegetables to prepare.

Chapter 16

"Great timing, just finished the veg!" Freddie laughed, as Connor plonked 20 coins on the table, and beamed. "I'm a professional busker! I couldn't stop people giving me money."

"That's great. What happened?"

"Well, I played all my songs—"

"With Leech, you eejit!"

"Oh! Yes, sorry. Well, an hour after you went, he left with two blokes pulling a cart loaded up with clothes and stuff. I followed him back to his office and they took it all inside. Then the men left, but Leech is still there." Connor struggled for a second. "Freddie, what's going to happen? Are you going to stay here and live like a king in Devon?" Connor's eyes betrayed his concern.

"No, mate. As soon as we sort this legal thing,

Mingoe and Jack can have my share and I'm coming home with you for Christmas."

A relieved smile lit up Connor's face.

Pepys praised Connor's latest meal. "Another conquest, although you know I like my vegetables cut smaller."

Freddie silently apologised and Connor mouthed back, 'No worries', as he set about teaching Samuel's guests the theme to the Pied Piper.

Freddie left the musicians to it, but as he lit the street candle, Billy Jenks tore around the corner and ran into him, wrapping his arms tightly around his lost friend.

"Billy, I can't breathe!" Freddie laughed, struggling for air. "How are you?"

"I thought you was dead," said the small boy standing back and wiping tears from his huge eyes. "I thought I'd never... I thought..."

"It's fine, Billy. I'm back. We've got to sort some things out and we'll need your help."

"Anything, Freddie. Oh! The message is, Boggy will be back next week."

"I wish it was sooner. So you've kept away from that gang?"

"Yes, I always slip past. I've only been caught the once and you lot saved me. I've just seen 'em take another one as I came here. They was dragging this girl towards Dice Quay."

"That's terrible. What will they do with her?"

"I don't know," replied Billy. "But they'll never sell her 'coz she's a witch."

"A witch? How do you know?"

"'Coz she had blue hair. All over one side of her head. They'll have to cut it all off and… What's wrong?"

Freddie didn't move. He wanted time to turn back and delete the last thing he'd heard. He swallowed hard.

"How old do you think she was?"

"Your age."

"What was she wearing?"

"That's another funny thing. Breeches! On a girl! And big boots like a fisherman. Maybe they'll sell her to the Navy to scare away the Dutch." Billy tried to make Freddie laugh with no success.

Freddie began to run towards Dice Quay. "Follow me!" he called to Billy.

Catching their breath in the shadows, Freddie and Billy watched the warehouse. The doors opened and light spilled out, revealing the sight Freddie dreaded more than anything. Lashed to the wooden post at the bottom of a steep staircase, was Ruby. She was shouting and thrashing about. Bob Packer tied a scarf around her mouth to suppress the noise and stood back alongside Aggie, as Old Ma Packer strode in to join them.

Freddie and Billy scuttled nearer the entrance

so they could hear. It was a warm, dark night and all attention was on the new arrival.

"I've never seen nothing like it," said Aggie, flicking her knife hopefully with her fingers. "Look at her, she's a sight."

"We'll have trouble shifting her, Ma," said Bob. "Who's going to want a blue-haired mopsy?"

"You're wrong, both of you. She's got spirit, she's strong, she'll sell for plenty, you mark my words." Old Ma coughed and spat. "And if they don't like blue hair, they'll chop it off. It's just dye, and it'll grow back proper." She lifted Ruby's chin. She was still screaming but only muffled sounds escaped.

"Yeah! She's a good 'un, look at the fire in her eyes. She reminds me of me when I was her age. I know plenty that'd like to meet this little princess. Get her a fancy dress from stock and put the word out we've got a diamond for sale." Two cronies undid the ropes and dragged Ruby upstairs as the warehouse door slammed shut.

Billy whispered, "I said she's a witch."

"She's not, Billy, she's my friend and we've got to save her before she's sold to someone. How can we get up to the higher floors?" They scanned the weather-boarded walls, covered in pitch to seal the wood against the elements. At both top ends of the long building were loading bays with small balconies that led to double doors. A strong horizontal beam jutted out, at the end of which was a metal pulley and a huge looped rope for lowering cargo down into waiting boats on the river end, or onto carts at the City end.

Freddie thought Billy looked like a crab scampering up the outside of the building, using footholds where the boards were uneven. He unhooked the rope and guided it to Freddie. Billy continued to the top and heaved as hard as he could. Freddie scrambled up, and they eventually stood panting by the double doors.

There was no lock, and Freddie pushed the left-hand door open, just wide enough for Billy to squeeze in and clear a tea chest that had been in the way. Freddie followed and closed the door. Light spilled up the staircase and from between the floorboards, making it easy to pick out a route to the top step. Bob's voice travelled up the building.

"Lock her in, and leave that scarf on. I don't wanna listen to her shouting all night. Tie her tight. She's a wriggler."

Freddie lowered his head through the gap and saw two men shove Ruby into a room on the floor below. They emerged a minute later and locked the door. One threw the key to Bob who was sitting with his back turned at a table a few metres away. Freddie whispered to Billy, "He's put the key on his desk. We'll just have to wait until he goes somewhere, then release Ruby."

"Ruby? Is that her name? She should have *red* hair, not blue," whispered Billy, smiling.

For the next hour the boys sat huddled in the dark, waiting for an opportunity. Freddie elaborated his *Treasure Island* tale for Billy.

"I wonder if you saw my dad out there? I bet you did. He 'aint big. He's like me, but older. It's been so long since he was taken. I hope I remember his face."

"You will, Billy. I'm positive." Freddie smiled. Then, deep in his mind, an idea began to form. It felt good, and it felt right. He hoped his plan would work out.

Toothless Aggie climbed the stairs with a fancy dress. "This is for Ma's new favourite. She's not to wear it yet, 'coz she'll mess it up before the viewings. Hang it nice so the creases fall out."

Bob put it on a hook and Aggie stood back admiringly. "I'd look nice in that."

"You? Look nice? With no teeth? You're dreaming."

Aggie stormed downstairs. He followed. "Take more than teeth and a fancy frock to turn *you* into a lady." There was a thud of metal into wood and a squeal of pain from Bob. "Ow! You devil. Stop throwing that thing at yer own people!"

"Well, stop saying I 'aint a lady then."

The boys waited a moment then tiptoed silently down. Billy went to Bob's desk to look for the key, and Freddie crossed to the door and whispered to Ruby.

"Ruby? It's Freddie. Are you OK? Can you hear me? Tap with your foot if—" Three loud taps interrupted him. "Great! Welcome to London! I promise I'll get you home for Christmas."

Why was Billy taking so long? Freddie could see the problem as soon as he reached the desk. No key! They searched frantically. Nothing!

"We can't find the key, Ruby. Freddie lay down and peered under the door. He could see her sitting tied by the waist to a wooden pillar. He had an idea and felt in his pocket. "I'll slide my multi-tool across the floor." He followed the line of a floorboard back and after three practice swings, he skimmed the tool under the door, hoping he'd aimed well.

Billy kept watch. "She's got a foot on it," he said. "How's she going to use it though?"

Freddie hadn't thought of that. But if anyone could find a way it would be Ruby.

They heard Bob's heavy footfall climbing the stairs. The boys scarpered back up and hid. Freddie saw the key dangling from Bob's belt, and it looked like he was settling down to sleep. "I'm going to guard the diamond," he shouted down.

Freddie made his way to the far end of the top floor where a second opening, identical to the one high above the river, looked down over the courtyard. He made sure the door was easily opened, and arranged the rope so a quick escape could be made. They waited until loud snores reached their ears from below. Bob had his feet up on the table and was lying back in his chair.

"It's impossible. We'll have to come back," whispered Freddie.

They silently descended on the rope and scuttled off into the darkness, narrowly avoiding the shrouded figure, who passed just metres away before entering the warehouse. Freddie felt a pang of fear.

"Not 'im again. It's that blighter with the hood," whispered Billy. "I owe him a knock or two." Freddie realised the events had to be linked: Ruby's capture, and the appearance of their long-time enemy. There were foes on all sides and it was getting harder and harder to outwit them.

Chapter 17

Saturday, September 1st, 1666

The households of Penn, Batten and Pepys were in chaos as everyone prepared for the annual outing to Bartholomew Fair.

Freddie just couldn't find a way of telling Connor about Ruby, knowing he'd be devastated at her capture. He needed his friend to be his normal self to divert Pepys with his food and music, leaving Freddie free to attempt the rescue.

Billy Jenks arrived early. Freddie sent him to watch the warehouse and follow Ruby wherever she was taken. "As soon as it gets dark we'll come and find a way to release her. Good luck."

Freddie did tell Mingoe and Jack what was going on. "We'll help, we can distract the gang whilst you rescue her. But you'll need something to open the door," said Jack. They refined their plan during the day, as they followed their masters through the clamour of the fair.

As preoccupied as Freddie was, he was still amazed by the sights. It was mesmerising. On the same fields where, a year ago, four plague pits had been filled, Bartholomew Fair was now packed with all kinds of attractions. There were running races, throwing the bar, wrestling, nine-pins and stoolball, a cross between cricket and baseball. There were also cock-fights, dogfights and bearbaiting. Snakes were draped around ladies' necks and tigers paced in tiny cages.

But by far the strangest sight, was a sailor leading a dodo on a rope. He charged a penny to stroke the large bird, which was extinct in the 20th century. How incredible! *A dodo!*

Watching a Punch and Judy type puppet show, Pepys roared his approval. "This Polichinello is the best that I ever saw." As the clever Polichinello tied the villain of the play to a tree whilst he slept and robbed his purse back, Mingoe, Jack and Freddie all had the same idea. They smiled at each other. *Now they just needed some rope!*

The scorching afternoon turned to evening, and the servants were sent home, having deposited their masters in a nearby tavern. It was midnight when the three friends arrived at the warehouse.

They found Billy hidden behind the signs on Dice

Quay offering ferries to Ipswich and King's Lynn. "I'm starving," whispered the boy. Jack passed him some leftovers and they retreated further along the shoreline to catch up.

"No sign of her," Billy told them. "Not unless she's shaved her hair and grown a beard. The only people in and out have been Packer's ugly lot."

"Thanks Billy. Has Bob still got the key on his belt?"

"Yes and I had a thought. I know one of the best lock picks in London. I could run and get him, if you like?"

"Will he come?" asked Freddie

"Of course, if there's a shilling in it."

"Tell him he can have anything he can carry from the warehouse." Billy nodded and ran off into the night. This change of plan sounded a safer option than tying Bob Packer up as he slept.

Once Freddie was in position on the top balcony, Jack made his way up, pulled by Mingoe using the looped rope from ground level. His job was to keep watch.

All was quiet inside and they inched their way down the stairs until they reached Ruby's cell. Bob was nowhere to be seen, but they could hear snoring from somewhere.

"Ruby! Are you awake?" Freddie whispered.

"You took your time!" a voice hissed back.

Freddie smirked to himself. "Are you all right?"

"Just about. I've cut through the rope, but I can't open the door. I've tried everything."

"Help's coming," Freddie told her.

"Listen," hissed Ruby. "The shrouded man. He's here as well. I've seen him. And he was at your house. He was the other side of the map in the vortex."

"What's a vortex?" whispered Jack.

"Ruby, Jack's here, we'll talk about it when you're free," said Freddie trying to stem the flow of awkward questions Jack would ask.

"OK, buddy, but watch out. This whole thing just gets weirder."

At least an hour passed waiting for Billy. Twice Freddie checked on Ruby and twice he checked the escape routes. It was long after a nearby church struck two o'clock, that they heard scraping sounds. A second later, Billy was standing holding the double doors open for his accomplice. Freddie expected a seasoned rogue to stride in and demand a fortune to pick the lock. Instead, a boy even smaller than Billy, with white blonde hair, stood smiling angelically.

"This is Percy, the best lock picker in London," whispered Billy wiping his nose.

"I am very pleased to make your acquaintance," Percy said in a high clear voice.

"Sshh!" everyone said at once. Percy's smile disappeared under the withering glare from Billy, and he too wiped his nose on his sleeve, as if it was catching.

Billy whispered, "The streets are busy for some reason, I don't know why. It's the middle of the night and people are on the move, taking their stuff with them!"

Freddie frowned. "That's weird. Jack, can you see what's happening? I'll take Percy down to Ruby's door," Freddie whispered.

Once there Percy examined it, and then simply tried the handle. "Just checking," he said in a cheeky whisper, before producing a metal spike with a hook on the end. With his ear to the door, he started fiddling the lock.

The noise increased from the surrounding streets, which were ridiculously busy for 3 o'clock in the morning. "What's happening?" Ruby whispered. "I can hear lots of movement outside."

"Nearly done, madam," Percy replied.

Jack whispered down, "There's people all along Thames Street, with carts and bundles." The lock made a clicking sound and Percy turned the handle. Ruby and Freddie rushed towards each other and hugged tightly. Their footsteps echoed in the silent warehouse, and immediately the sound of someone stirring from their sleep came from below. Everyone froze in panic.

"Is that you, Bluey?" came Bob's sleepy voice. "Is that Ma's favourite, stamping her feet? It's not feeding time yet, my gal. You just wait." His laugh echoed around the building. The others stayed completely still, but then came Mingoe's prearranged owl-call warning. The big doors opened and several gang members rushed in.

While Bob's attention was diverted, Freddie moved everyone swiftly up to the top floor. Things had just got more complicated with the arrival of the thugs. Two at a time could escape on the rope, but there were five of them, so Freddie sent Billy and Jack to the river end of the warehouse loft, and Ruby and Percy to the city end. He would follow when they were safely down.

Suddenly he could smell smoke. If the warehouse had caught fire, they were all done for. But as soon as Billy opened the double doors it was obvious something extraordinary was happening outside.

For a start it was no longer dark. They could clearly see Mingoe waving below. They all looked to their right. About 300 metres away they saw a shower of sparks shoot into the night sky from a burning warehouse. Beyond that all that could be seen were buildings spewing smoke, and a giant wall of flames.

Freddie gasped and looked at the others. Everyone was wide-eyed with horror. This was big! And Freddie knew exactly what was happening and what it meant.

"Go, go, go!" he said to Billy and Jack. He raced to the other end of the loft to help Ruby and Percy escape. The situation became much clearer looking out towards the city. About four streets to their left was a giant orange curtain of flames, sending sparks and burning embers up into the dark sky. Some fell nearby and Freddie could see they were sure to set light to the buildings next door. A strong warm wind was fanning the flames, and the streets below were full of frantic Londoners, racing away with whatever belongings they could carry.

"No way!" Ruby cried. "It's the Great Fire! Look!" She pointed at the warehouses that lined the river, which Freddie knew contained flammable stock like oil and brandy. They were covered in pitch that kept out the wet, but burned in an instant. One huge building had been engulfed in the short time they'd been watching.

Down below, the Packer gang were trying to rescue as much of their loot as possible. There were threatening people outside, stealing their carts and loading their own goods on instead. Freddie counted at least 15 disappear into the busy streets heading away from the fire. Other gang members were now down by the quay, throwing protesting ferryman into the water and stealing their boats.

Old Ma Packer and Bob were underneath Ruby and Percy's escape route. They heard her shout, "Get the girl, she's more valuable than all these dresses put together."

"But, Ma…"

"Now!" She strode off and Bob made for the door, cursing. The coast was clear. Freddie needed to think quickly.

"Percy, go with Ruby." Percy nodded at Freddie and grabbed the rope.

"You follow straight away," Ruby told Freddie.

"I will! But I've got to delay Bob finding out you've gone."

Shouting came from downstairs, and Freddie raced back inside. Bob was instructing a dozen men. "Grab the gold and silver and head for St Paul's. Just load the best stuff, and look lively."

Bob headed upstairs, lighting his way with a lantern. *I know how to stop him!* Freddie thought. He tiptoed over to dozens of small barrels stacked by the stairwell. Would he be able to lift one? He bent down and took a firm grip on the nearest keg.

Freddie caught a glimpse of Aggie as she called up, "Why bother, Bob? Just let her burn." The toothless girl then heaved a huge sack of silver candlesticks onto her shoulders and trudged off.

"I'll tell Ma you said that," he laughed.

As he neared the top of the staircase, his lantern shone across the floor, revealing the open cell.

"What the…?"

"Are you missing someone?" said Freddie, launching the first of his barrels. It missed, but shattered on the floor and the contents spewed outwards, producing a strong smell of alcohol.

"You again? The boy who jumps into the earth.

I'll get you!" A second barrel smashed harmlessly and Freddie cursed his aim. He had to hit Bob with one or the man would just climb up and grab him. The third and fourth missed too, as Bob easily sidestepped the falling missiles. But the fifth caught him a glancing blow on the shoulder, causing him to drop the lantern, which instantly set light to the spilled alcohol, spreading a sheet of purple flame all around his feet. He looked up as Freddie launched one last barrel. Bob caught it like a goalkeeper, before staggering backwards, tripping on a broken keg and falling down the burning open staircase, screaming as he bounced down the hard wooden steps.

Freddie fled to the city end of the warehouse loft. His disbelieving eyes took in the great swathe of flame across the nearby streets. He leaped out, grabbed the rope and controlled his descent into a heap of abandoned dresses.

Ruby and Percy grabbed him and dragged him into the shadows where the others were waiting.

They had no time to celebrate. Bob limped around the corner with a large cut on his forehead, ranting at the top of his voice, "Where is he? He's stolen the girl! That's the second time he's vanished on me."

"Never mind 'im! Get this cart to St Paul's," shouted Ma. "Now!"

"But, Ma… It's the boy!"

"I don't care about no boy, they're ten a penny. You've

lost my blue-haired beauty!" Explosions sounded from inside as barrels of brandy ignited. Within seconds the whole building was ablaze.

They watched Bob limp away with a loaded cart, and once it was safe, Ruby and her rescuers skirted the shoreline, away from the disaster towards the Tower of London.

The Great Fire had indeed started, and one of the most famous events in history was playing out in front of them. Catching their breath on Tower Hill, and watching the orange skyline dance with increasing menace, Freddie and Ruby exchanged a look.

Speechless, they stared at the chaos.

Chapter 18

Sunday, September 2nd, 1666

At 3 am, Connor and the household were woken by Jane the maid, warning about the fire. But Pepys told everyone to go back to bed saying there was no danger. Connor was so sleepy he said 'Goodnight' to Freddie's empty bed, assuming his friend was asleep when he didn't answer.

Soon after, Freddie returned with Ruby and the three friends were reunited. Connor was stunned at hearing what they'd been through, and was ecstatic at seeing Ruby again, and very relieved he hadn't been in the warehouse. Dangling on a rope four storeys up wasn't for him. He would have messed up the whole escape. They hadn't slept a wink by the time Pepys rose again at seven, and whilst staring at the building wall of flames in the distance, Connor introduced Ruby to him as another refugee from the *Hispaniola* crew.

"Ruby you say? But why have you blue—?" A frantic knock at the door interrupted the questions and jolted everyone into action. It was Will Hewer, a stick-thin man, and another of Pepys's secretaries who arrived with news. He gathered everyone in the hall.

"My father's house was lost in minutes. There was nothing we could do. It was like watching paper burn."

"Yes, yes, but how did it start?" said Pepys impatiently. Clearly expecting a little more sympathy from his master, the young man replied, "Some say a baker's shop caught light in Pudding Lane, or the Star Inn on Fish Street Hill. Others say the French or Dutch have invaded and set light to the city. Rumours fly like sparks from the fire. Everyone's blaming everyone else."

Connor wanted to reveal the truth, but it would sound deeply suspicious if he said, 'Actually it started in Thomas Farriner's bakery shop in Pudding Lane and then spread to the Star Inn.'

Hewer carried on. "The church bells sounded a warning, but it's Sunday, so people thought they rang for morning service. Mayor Bludworth was shown the fire when it started. He said it was of little consequence and would soon burn itself out. Within an hour a hundred houses disappeared and three hundred more in the next. It's spreading so quickly because the strong wind is blowing westwards and causing sparks to fly, with no way to stop them. All the warehouses are burning along Thames Street and their contents lost. People can't get between them to fetch water from the river to fight the flames."

"We need to organise," said Pepys. "I'll go to the king at once. Where's Bludworth now?"

"He went back to bed, so they say," said Hewer, who sank down on a chair, shaking his head in disbelief.

Pepys calmly gave instructions to everyone. "Jane, help Elizabeth pack our smaller valuables into trunks. Be ready to leave at short notice. The fire is still a long way off and blowing away from us, but that might change, and we must be ready.

"Fred, you and your blue-haired friend should go and help fight the fire. Make yourselves busy saving who and what you can. Remember to send word of any developments that may affect this house. We must save Seething Lane at all costs. Connor and I will go to the king and report on the mayor's hopelessness. We'd best go to White Hall by river from Tower Wharf. Fred, fetch my belt."

"Your belt, sir?"

"Yes, the black belt that hangs on my closet door. Quickly now."

Freddie handed the belt to Pepys, who was now standing over a casket in his library. He unlocked it and revealed hundreds of gold coins. He began loading them into the secret pouches built into the leather.

"Three hundred fit in here, Fred. Emergency money. What else can they test me with? First the plague, now this."

On his way out, Freddie whispered to Connor, "Good luck, and watch out for the shrouded man, he's here somewhere."

Connor looked worried. "What shall I say to the king?"

"Just be yourself, mate, take him some mince pies. You'll be fine. See you later and stay safe, we've got to get back home for Christmas, remember."

Pepys blustered back into the hall. "Why are you blathering about Christmas?" he said. "Get on with you, Fred, there are houses burning."

Ruby nodded encouragement to Connor. Even she looked a little tense, and who could blame her? Once again Freddie and his map had plunged them all into a life-or-death situation. This latest one would take some beating, Freddie thought.

Mingoe and Jack were released from their duties and they too raced towards the huge pall of smoke that spiralled away from the streets in front of them. The quartet battled against the tide of escaping human traffic to the heart of the fire and its mayhem.

Freddie saw some amazing sights: people too ill to walk were carried in their beds; hand-carts and animals had precious possessions strapped tightly aboard; and families moved in clusters, with children staggering under impossible weights, urged on by frantic parents who'd survived the plague but once again risked losing everything.

Ruby spied an abandoned shop with a stock of wooden buckets and they carried as many as they could towards the smoke. She was struck by the faces of the exhausted families. They were walking in silence with dead eyes. Occasionally they stopped, readjusted their burdens, and looked back at their homes and streets, which lay ruined. The fierce light of the blaze was aglow on their faces.

She heard snippets of news. "St Clements has burned, I saw it fall with my own eyes," one old man said. "Everyone in Canon Street had put their things inside the church, thinking the stone wouldn't burn, but it did I tell you, I saw it!"

It was surprising to Ruby that only a tiny number of people were trying to stop the fire spreading. Turning into Fish Street Hill, the heat from the raging inferno hit them. It was a hot September morning anyway, but coupled with the searing temperature generated by the still smouldering ruins of St Michael's Church, it combined to flush their faces and prickle their skin even at 100 metres.

At last there were signs of organised help. For an hour or so they joined a human chain passing buckets of water, the contents of which were launched at endangered buildings, hoping to stop the fire's advance but it was a hopeless effort as the sparks were now leaping six houses at a time, easily igniting the tinder-dry dwellings that had baked during the long hot summer.

The water chain gave up when a row of houses they'd thoroughly doused simply exploded in a fireball. They fell back, defeated, and gathered around a soldier who was still dressed in his nightshirt, stained with soot and sweat. He'd sent his family away with just one sack of possessions after they'd watched their house collapse. "But I saved my boots," he told Ruby with a hollow laugh. "These wooden shutters on shops spread the flames, then the stock inside ignites, like that." He clicked his fingers. As if to illustrate his point, an Apothecary's shop exploded nearby, showering the surrounding area with burning debris and setting several new fires going.

"Rip down the shutters! Perhaps that will slow this devil," shouted the soldier already heaving at the wooden façade of a butcher's shop. The intrepid band of 50 or so men, women and children set about tearing off the panels all along Canon Street.

Ruby had splinters and cut hands, but all their work proved pointless when a surge in the wind fuelled the fire's advance. It drove the brave fighters back and Canon Street was lost.

With their throats stinging from the smoke, they

retreated and found themselves walking silently past the ruins of Philpot Lane. Mingoe and Jack surveyed the smouldering wreckage of Alconbury House. Sir Bradley Roast's gift was a ruin, save for the stone frame of the bay window that stood as a mournful reminder.

"You've still got the farm in Devon," Ruby offered.

Mingoe and Jack stared at the shell of the building that would have been their home.

"It's my belief that we are destined not to inherit Sir Bradley's estate," Mingoe simply said. "It's always felt too good to be true."

It was a truly distressing site from the prow of the wherry that carried Connor and Pepys upstream. Samuel reeled off street and church names that he could see lost from their position, mid-river, whilst Connor made hurried notes.

The ferryman was going as fast as he could, not only because Pepys had said it was the king's business, but because he would be able to charge a fortune. "What was a two-shilling fare yesterday is ten today," he chortled happily, smirking greedily at Connor.

Then London Bridge loomed and Pepys gasped. "The only reason it's not spreading onto the bridge is because the houses on the north end burned down in the last blaze, so a break was created. *A firebreak!* That's what we need in the city. We must pull down houses in the path of the flames to stop them spreading. We've no hope otherwise."

On sped the boat, helped by the incoming tide, and they eventually outpaced the flames. Connor looked back at the huge pall of smoke that rose into the otherwise bright sky, and then spread like a fan as the wind caught it and sent it westwards. Nothing stood a chance of survival down in the tightly packed streets of the old city. Rocked by plague, now mocked by flame.

The sniggering boatman deposited them at Privy Stairs, which was the quickest way of getting to the king's private quarters.

Pepys and a very nervous, sweaty Connor, found Charles and his brother James, Duke of York standing on a high balcony with telescopes trained on the fire about three kilometres away.

They didn't take their eyes from the disaster, as the king asked, "What's happening, Pepys? Pray God you bring some good news."

"Your Majesty, I fear not. The fire is completely out of control and will only be stopped by creating firebreaks. We pray the wind drops, and stops fanning the flames as it does at present, but we need to pull down, or with gunpowder, blow up strategic sections in the path of the blaze. One or two houses will not be enough: the flames leap ten at a time in places. Drastic and brave action is needed now to stop the loss of the whole city."

"Agreed, and I shall instruct it so." The king signalled to a scribe who started on an order dictated by one of his entourage.

"Tell me how it comes to this?" said James.

"My information is that the fire started in Pudding Lane, and Mayor Bludworth was called to direct operations, but said it was of little consequence and went home to bed. An hour later, 100 houses were gone, and every hour the rate increases three or five fold."

The king scoffed in disgust. "Tell Bludworth to follow our orders to the letter. My brother will take charge later. Then we will plan for tomorrow. Fetch me something to eat, I'm starving."

Connor was walking towards the king before he knew what he was doing, and retrieved from his satchel the muslin-wrapped mince pies he had made yesterday.

"Your Majesty." He bowed and offered them to the king and duke. They were slightly taken aback but were so hungry that they took two each and ate them quickly before taking a third.

"Very good, boy. Your name?"

"Connor Massey, sir," he said, flushing with embarrassment.

"Another Irishman, Pepys? Where do you find them all? Are there any children left in Ireland?"

"I'm glad you approve, Your Majesty." He gestured for Connor to retreat. "I will take your orders to Bludworth, sir, and see to it personally that he follows them exactly." With that he took the signed and sealed scroll handed to him, and they began to back away.

"Not so fast," said the king. "Are there pies left in that cloth, Mr Massey?"

"Yes, sir, Your Majesty." He offered the last two mince pies to the royal brothers. The king ruffled Connor's neat hair and turned back to the serious business of fire watching. "A guinea for Mr Massey," said the king, and a clerk stepped forward and pressed a gold coin in his hand. Connor hated people ruffling his hair but was not going to reprimand the King of England for doing so. *What's a guinea?* he asked himself. *I'm going to keep this forever*, he thought as he neatened his fringe.

As they rode in a carriage back towards the flames Pepys said, "I am mightily pleased with your cooking, your music, and your company, Connor. When these flames dampen we will send the king some more of your pies to remind him what loyal subjects we are. Now, stay close as we look for Bludworth. That man has made a very grave mistake. His stupidity will echo down through the years, you mark my words."

Chapter 19

At midday, Connor witnessed the confrontation between Pepys and Bludworth. It was very loud and very public. After deserting their carriage, which was unable to negotiate the fleeing tide of humanity, Connor was told the mayor was near Canon Street. Although still wearing his wig, he was a shattered man. He begged Pepys, "Lord, What can I do? I am spent! People will not obey me."

"These are the king's direct orders."

"I *have* been pulling down houses," said Bludworth, reading the demand. "But the fire overtakes us." The mayor fussily rearranged his clothes, put his frock coat on and marched away saying, "I need to freshen myself. I've been up all night."

What sort of leader does that? Connor thought.

Pepys handed the king's order to a militia sergeant,

then rushed off, barking to Connor, "Keep up, boy," and turning up towards Lombard Street to avoid a ferocious inferno blocking their route.

Connor laboured around abandoned furniture that clogged the already packed alleys. He could see it was acting like a fuse from one side of a lane to the other. The flames didn't even have to be blown, they crossed on stepping stones from bed to table to opposite house.

Up ahead a group were loading elderly patients from a convent into wagons. Connor was thrilled and Pepys gasped when he saw Ruby, Freddie, Mingoe and Jack covered in dirt, sweat and blood, pulling doors off their hinges to use as stretchers.

"Well, my word! My brave souls! What heroics! You're doing great work here, but remember, your priority is to stop the flames reaching Seething Lane," Pepys added selfishly. They nodded dutifully, and turned their attention back to the real business of saving lives.

"Can I stay and help?" asked Connor.

"If you must, but be careful of those fingers. Don't let your music suffer for a lost cause." *Pepys really could be extremely self-centred*, thought Connor.

"Hello, mate," said Freddie.

"I met the king," Connor smiled. "He loved the mince pies."

Freddie smiled back. "I told you." He looked at the flags on the Royal Exchange to see how strong the winds were still.

"Come on, Conman, help me with this stretcher." Ruby was standing over a frail man laid flat on a wooden door. "Grab the other end," she rasped, parched and hoarse from smoke inhalation. Connor hoped she hadn't suffered any lasting damage.

An hour later the flames turned the corner from St Nicholas Lane, as the last patient was safely evacuated. One by one the shops ignited like fireworks in a display. Pigeons roosting on upper window ledges stayed until the last second, then took off, only for some of them to leave it too late, falling to earth scorched and featherless.

Freddie called, "Let's move back."

The exhausted posse washed and drank from the conduit at Cornhill. The roar of the fire hundreds of metres away was a constant reminder of the calamity. The terrible crashes as houses collapsed sent thousands more sparks into the hot air, speeding fresh dangers on to new targets. The relentless march now spread out in clusters over at least a kilometre, and was expanding rapidly.

"Let's get back to Seething Lane and rest for a while. We can't help anyone in this state," said Mingoe wearily. Freddie could hardly put one foot in front of the other and everyone else looked spent. As they set off, a strange column of carts approached, piled high. Freddie rushed everyone into cover behind a low wall. The Packers were scouring deserted houses and shops for valuables. They'd lost the warehouse on Dice Quay, they'd mislaid the blue-haired beauty who was worth a fortune, but they were still in business, and doing extremely well by the look of things.

"Two more loads Ma wants tonight," Bob commanded, as the column passed their hiding place. "Then each man has a pick of a piece to take home. So choose well, brothers. The better you lift, the better to choose from." His laugh was echoed by his mercenary band.

A soldier in a bright scarlet uniform rode past and asked, "Where are you taking all these goods?"

"To safety, Sir," Bob replied in a mock-honest tone. "Away from the Dutch, sir. We caught them lighting a church and we saw them off. It's the Dutch that's caused all this."

"The Dutch! You're mad!" said the soldier. "I'll be back with more men to arrest you. Thieving scoundrels. How dare you!"

A flash of metal spun through the air and sank deep into the soldier's hard leather waistcoat. He fell from his horse, and the toothless grinning Aggie scuttled to retrieve her knife, before wiping it clean and grabbing the bridle of the charger and leading it away. Freddie gasped at the cold-blooded violence he'd just witnessed.

"Nice bit of meat there, girl," said Bob pointing at

the chestnut mare.

"Yeah, she'll cook up lovely. I'm starving."

The column sped away and Ruby raced over to the soldier. "He's still alive – *just!* Where shall we take you?"

"The Artillery... Company. New... Artillery Gardens. Our surgeon is there. Stop the..." At which point the man passed out.

"Stop the what?" said Connor, panicking.

"Stop the blood, I think," said Ruby, pulling off the soldier's leather jacket and packing it tight against the wound.

A carriage tore down the street, followed immediately by the loose chestnut mare who must have escaped Aggie's grasp. Freddie and Mingoe slowed both down and asked the driver to take the soldier. "What, right up there? It's going to cost you."

"How much?" said Ruby directly

"Well..." He rolled his eyes.

"*How much?*"

"Yesterday it would've been a shilling, but prices have gone up. Today it's ten shillings."

"*Ten* shillings, that's ridiculous," said Freddie

"Take it or leave it," said the coachman, gathering the reins.

"A guinea!" said Connor. "A golden guinea from the king." He showed the sparkling coin to the driver, whose eyes lit up.

"That'll do nicely big'un. For that I'll get you there twice as quick."

Mingoe and Jack said they'd go with the soldier and loaded him carefully inside, whilst Ruby tied his horse to the carriage, which then sped off north towards Bishopsgate.

At Seething Lane, Jane handed out fresh uniforms. "Pepys said to spoil you," she smiled. One minute he was extremely selfish, then kind and generous the next. Like the flames outside, he changed direction with the wind.

At sunset, a messenger summoned Pepys to attend the royal barge on the river. Gathering all his notes in a satchel, he called Connor to go with him for his second river trip of the day. "What delights can you take for the king?" he added as an afterthought.

"I'll find something, sir." Connor rushed off to the kitchen to find some treats.

"May we come, sir?" Freddie asked.

"If there's room, and if Ruby wears a cloth cap to hide her, err, peculiarity." He strode off, with his excited staff following behind.

A naval 'tilt' boat stood by Tower Wharf ready for Pepys, and although it had a sail, the extra power of Freddie and Ruby on the oars helped to row faster upstream. Freddie had no idea where they found the energy. Adrenalin probably.

The sky was like a painting. A massive orange and

red arc crowned the city above the rooftops that sagged and crashed with sickening regularity. As they fell, sparks flew tens of metres into the sky, standing out against the giant pall of rising black smoke.

The river was packed with traffic. Barges, wherries, hoys, ketches and lighters, boats of all shapes and sizes, crisscrossed the river, taking people and goods to the safety of the South Bank. Around them floated the scattered goods of people who'd piled their escape craft too high, and had capsized or thrown things overboard to stay afloat. Connor watched dozens of people wade into the river on the Southwark side and retrieve valuables from the water. *Even in a disaster, some people still found a way to make money*, he thought.

For once there was no queue to get under London Bridge as the majority of river traffic was running across, not along its length. As soon as they were through they spotted the royal barge with the gold of its paintwork reflecting the flames onshore.

Pepys's boat was safely moored alongside and as he updated the king and the Duke of York who sat on the elevated stern, Ruby stared in awe at the royal brothers, surrounded by ranks of advisers.

"Thank you. The Duke of York will assume command tomorrow. We make our plan as we watch. Tell Pepys your ideas." Charles indicated James to speak.

"We will have eight stations around the city. Each

with a commander, 30 soldiers and 100 strong men to carry out their orders. We will create firebreaks to slow the progress. We have ordered the water engines from Deptford and Woolwich to attend, and positioned all persons, capable to assist in the preservation of the Tower. What would you add to this?"

"Only, Your Highness, that your soldiers patrol in strength, to deter the many looters who take advantage of the mayhem. Just an hour ago my household saved one of your horse guards who was attacked by a plundering mob."

"Indeed?" The king's eyes picked out Connor's face in the light. "Ah! My mince pie magician, have you something to cheer me, on this most desperate of nights?"

"Yes, Your Majesty." Connor stood to take his offerings to the king, but the boat wobbled so alarmingly that he settled for passing the satchel along. Beautiful quince jam tarts were unwrapped before Charles and James.

"You excel yourself again, Mr Massey. I will run out of golden guineas at this rate." And as the satchel was passed back, a clerk put in a coin in grateful recognition. Connor's face flushed an even deeper crimson.

A silence fell over the entire group; soldiers, sailors, servants, nobles and royalty alike, as they stared at the unbelievable sight, unable to take it all in. Opposite them, just to the right of Swan Staires, the mighty roof of Fishmonger's Hall collapsed in a lengthy salvo. It caused the largest volley of sparks that anyone had yet seen. After the gasps of shock and the cries of anguish died away, the silence returned.

And then...

A boy from another time, with a recorder he hadn't wanted to keep, played a lament from another world. The simple haunting tune, sounded over the water, and provided the perfect soundtrack to the catastrophe before them, and captured exactly how they all felt.

Even the king had a tear in his eye.

Chapter 20

Monday, September 3rd, 1666

At 4 am Freddie and Ruby helped Hewer load a cart lent by Batten, who had moved his wealth yesterday. The destination was Sir William Ryder's house in the village of Bethnal Green, just outside the city, who was sheltering valuables for wealthy friends. In the kitchen, Connor worked round the snoring cook who awoke grumpily. "Be quiet, boy. You clack and crash and split my head with your thumpings."

I'm doing all your work as well as my own, Connor thought. But she was asleep again before he could answer.

Billy Jenks rounded the corner and leaned breathlessly against the cart. "Message for you, sir," he panted. "From a fancy man called James. 'Tell Pepys to bring his "ee-roic" staff to St Dunstan's and report to Lord…' *Someone!* Bell- sum'fing. Soon as you can."

"Lord Belasyse you mean boy. Bell – ass – size." Pepys drummed out the name.

"Yeah, *him!* And this fancy man, James, said Mr Massey was 'specially needed'."

Just then Connor emerged from the front door with separate muslin wraps containing packed lunches for everyone. Pepys clapped his hands. "Come Mr Massey, we have an appointment with the Duke of York."

"Is that a tavern?" Billy asked Freddie.

Freddie chuckled warmly. "No, Billy, the Duke of York is the king's brother."

"It can't be, he was in shirt-sleeves pulling down houses."

"That's him all right," Freddie confirmed. Billy stared in wonder.

"He gave me a shilling n'all, look!"

"You're a royal messenger now," smiled Ruby.

Billy led them to St Dunstan's, close by the ruins of Dice Quay. The Duke of York and several dozen men were pulling down the walls of a row of houses on Idol Lane between the church and the fire, hoping to cause a big enough gap that the flames couldn't cross.

"Our main aim is to stop the fire reaching the Tower of London," Lord Belasyse boomed authoritatively. Six-hundred throusand pounds of gunpowder have been taken there for safekeeping, but if the wind changes and those barrels catch, never a sound like it will have been heard in this world, or a hole dug as deep. Each command post is creating a firebreak, but the flames that were in three large patches yesterday, have joined to create one mighty force—"

"My lord," interrupted a soldier on horseback.

"What is it?"

"From Southwark, sir, a message to say the fire is caught on the wind and now crossing the river. In Horseshoe Alley, sir, a blaze started which was dealt with, but now the wind is so strong that the terror can cross the water!"

"When will someone ride up with good news?" Lord Belasyse said to the heavens.

From out of the smoke ahead of Freddie, marched a crocodile of uniformed schoolboys under the eagle eye of a master. They came to an exact halt as commanded.

"I'm John Dobson, the Dean of Westminster," said a wiry man. "And m'boys are here to assist in whatsoever way. Tell us what to do."

Belasyse nodded. "My only orders are, fetch water, water, and *more* water. Put three boys with each man along Idol Lane and guard this church and the Tower with all your might."

"Indeed, my lord, we will try."

"And thank you. I prayed for good news and you appeared. I will try that again. Keep London safe, brave lads."

The schoolboys cheered.

The Duke of York commanded Connor to his side. "Supply me with the tools I need in turn," he smiled. Already sweating with the heat of the day, and now with the fire only a short distance away, Connor was almost purple. He stood with a long wooden pole in one hand and a bucket of water in the other. The pole had a great hook on the end with which James could pull away walls and joists to collapse buildings. When not using that, he swapped it for a long metal crowbar that Connor held alternately. He watched the Westminster boys run backwards and forwards, whilst Ruby and Freddie teamed up with William Taswell, a lad with energy every bit as inexhaustible as their own.

"I was up all night writing about what I saw yesterday," Taswell told Ruby. "I've kept a record of all I remember."

Freddie stopped abruptly and stared at the ground, "The diary!" he whispered. "I've forgotten to get it! Keep an eye on Connor, please make sure he drinks something, and—"

"I'll look after him, don't worry. Just be careful."

Freddie sprinted away as fast as he could. *How could I have forgotten?* he thought.

The streets were less crowded today, but he still had to negotiate loaded carts and bewildered families blocking passageways. A fierce stitch bent him double, but calling on all his strength, Freddie dragged himself onwards, amazed at the progress of the blaze north towards Cornhill. He weaved through now-familiar turnings and shortcuts until he burst out of the alley by John Cade's shop, which was still standing, but less than half an hour from destruction. Several exhausted men were stacking books on carts. Freddie raced inside where he found the master binder, William Richardson, pulling volumes of books off shelves. The man was in a daze.

"Pepys! Ah! Yes, it's here. *Somewhere!* Look at the spine, it says 'Journal III'." Richardson's exhausted voice almost faded completely. Freddie set about searching through cabinets and haphazardly stacked piles. He thought he must have missed it and would have to start again when suddenly, in front of his eyes, lay a book with a beautiful calf-brown cover and a ridged spine, simply stating 'Journal III'. He picked out the book from midway up a stack and turned to the first page where he saw the familiar words he had read to Connor and Ruby: 'This morning it rained...' *How London could do with that now*, Freddie thought.

He tucked it safely in his waistband at the back where it was held securely by his belt, then helped the men stack the remaining stock on carts.

"Where are you taking them?" asked Freddie as they watched the last cart pull away.

"One of our best customers is the vicar of Stepney. I pray God they're safe there."

"I hope so t—" began Freddie, but was stopped by a thunderous crack as the building behind Cade's shop sagged and crumpled in a plume of sparks. The sky showered lethally sharp, burning splinters that fell and bounced around them. One fist-sized block struck Richardson on the head and Freddie leaped to brush it away before it set light to his shirt. Bad memories of the Thyangboche fire crowded Freddie's mind as he led Richardson to a deserted tavern, where he tended his cut with a rag from the bar.

Richardson winced, talking quickly to take his mind off the pain. "One of the carters said the General Letter Office burned at midday, and two hours later the Exchange was lost, with the shopkeepers struggling to carry out their fancy stock. It is the end of London as it is known," William mournfully reflected.

Freddie nodded sadly. "Where will you go?"

"I will follow my books and stay with them. I must see them safe, until we set up shop again. They are my livelihood, but also my family, and my children."

Above the constant background roar of collapsing buildings, fierce shouting sounded from outside. Freddie opened the door and saw a middle-aged, well-dressed man being pelted with stones and debris by a group of 20 drunken youths.

"French scum," slurred one, hefting a cobble at the man who thankfully ducked to avoid the missile.

"Burn our city would you? I'll show you!" yelled

another as he wielded a split post like a javelin. Luckily his aim was off, and it thumped into the wall near Freddie.

"*Je suis innocent*, I am inno..." This time a stone caught his shoulder and the Frenchman collapsed in pain. The mob sensed triumph and moved in to finish the man. "Get him!" they screamed.

Freddie ran and dragged the Frenchman by the arm through the door of the tavern. Richardson piled tables and chairs against the now-locked door. Freddie started blocking the windows, using the shutters and then upending a table against each one. The Frenchman gathered his strength and joined in, thanking his saviours. "*Merci!* Thank you, *mes amis.*"

"We can't hold them off forever. Let's try the back," said Richardson.

The door and windows were being pounded by the mob and they would soon smash their way in. The back of the tavern was a maze of dark corridors and dingy rooms, with no logical route to the rear. Eventually the Frenchman shouted, "*Ici. Voici la porte.*"

"Careful!" shouted Freddie. "They might have come round."

They opened the door cautiously onto a squalid yard full of barrels and broken tables. If one spark landed here, the whole street would go up. They blocked the rear tavern door to delay any pursuit, but the back gate was completely inaccessible. They piled chairs on a table and scampered up the high wall, sitting astride the top to help Richardson, who was still holding the rag to his head.

They dropped into the alley and listened. Suddenly screams from the raging gang filled the deserted tavern as they searched high and low for the Frenchman, who had fresh panic in his eyes. "*Rapidement*! Quickly, quickly!"

"This way!" whispered Freddie, who instead of running along the alley and perhaps into trouble, tested the gates of the yards opposite. At the third attempt one gave way and they barged through the back door of a dress shop and through to the street beyond.

Richardson shook hands with them both, and mumbling his goodbyes headed for the sanctuary of Stepney, still mopping his scalp.

"*Merci, mon ami. Mon braves.*" The man bowed and shook Freddie's hand. "Pascal. *Mon nom est Pascal. Toi?*" The dark-haired man pointed at Freddie.

"Freddie, *monsieur*. Freddie Malone. Aah! I think we *still* have trouble." The mob weren't finished. Two or three of them emerged onto the street a hundred metres away with the fire behind them. Freddie and Pascal looked at each other for inspiration as the first stones skittered towards them from the rapidly swelling group. Luckily still out of range, they advanced at a jog, confident that this time they would have their Frenchman. But from behind Freddie and Pascal, a new sound emerged.

Atop a huge black charger, an officer held Richardson tightly as fifteen thundering horses and their blue-coated, sword-wielding riders from the King's Horseguards swept down Finch Lane and routed the drunken apprentices. They scattered in the path of the hooves and the expert blows delivered by the mounted soldiers. The entire bunch were now either running for their lives towards the fire, or lying nursing wounds far worse than they'd inflicted on Pascal.

The Frenchman fell to his knees, exclaiming his relief and thanks. "*Mon Dieu!*" he repeated several times, clasping Freddie's hand with a grateful grip.

The leading officer, in his tricorn hat, who was carrying a beaming Richardson in front of him, rode up and deposited the bookbinder on the cobbles next to Freddie.

"Sir, you're French?" boomed the officer in a voice that could probably be heard in Paris."

"*Oui, monsieur.* Yes I am."

"Then, sir, bonjour. And for your own protection, I will take you to the Spanish Embassy. They're kindly looking after foreign guests who encounter *trouble*, from certain ill-informed sections of our society."

He extended a hand, and in one single move pulled Pascal up and into the position just vacated by Richardson. "My name is De Vere. I command the 'Blues and Royals' for the king." Then looking at Freddie he said, "On his behalf, I thank you, sir, for aiding this gentleman. If only we had a thousand like you in this lawless city. Your name, sir, for our records?"

"He is Freddie Malone," said Pascal, waving his thanks once again, as the officer spurred his horse on, calling over his shoulder. "Thank you again, Mr Malone." The riders stormed past, all tipping their hats, as their mounts thundered on the cobbles under their mighty feet.

"Well, well. That's quite enough excitement for one day," said Richardson, and the pair walked as calmly as possible on slightly wobbly legs to the corner of Grace Church Street, where they shook hands.

"How's your head?" asked Freddie.

"My head? Ha! I'd completely forgotten. But now you mention it, yes! It stings rather. I shall get it bathed in Stepney, as I tell our story. How many shall I say attacked us? I don't want to exaggerate."

"It was a least one, maybe even two hundred!" Freddie replied with a smile and a wink.

"Oh! It was more than that, surely!" Richardson laughed, showing a side of his character he hadn't displayed up to now. "I think I'll tell the truth, after all, that is impressive enough, don't you think? Not bad for an old bookworm and a brave servant boy. I hope to see you again, Freddie, when all this is over. Remember me to your master. He can settle his bill at Stepney Church. Farewell."

Chapter 21

Everyone except Freddie had accompanied the Duke of York on his tour of command posts and were returning to Cheapside from Clifford's Inn, with Connor carried on horseback next to James. The others had to battle on foot through Ludgate against a fresh tide of refugees spilling from Alsatia, where Billy lived.

As they approached St Paul's, Mingoe spotted Aggie and Bob Packer perched on the scaffolding, sending boys out to rob the vulnerable. As soon as soldiers began to patrol the open area around the cathedral, the thieves disappeared.

It was not only booksellers who were transferring their stock into the crypt. Ruby overheard a woman with three sacks say, "This is the fifth time I've moved all my bits, but the fire keeps a'coming."

"What are they charging you?" Ruby asked.

"A shilling a day upfront, or a pound for a month. They say it'll be, safe as houses. Well, my house burned down yesterday, so I hope it's safer than that!" Laughing ironically, the woman shuffled forward in the queue. Ruby doubted whether she'd ever see her precious sacks again.

She led Mingoe and Jack round to the north side where there was another entrance to the crypt. Mingoe pointed to a procession of tea chests being furtively lifted onto carts, which left every few minutes.

"I bet they're opening people's goods, transferring it into their own chests and stealing it out of this side," said Ruby.

"The only way to prove it would be to get into the crypt and watch it happening," said Mingoe.

"How would we do that?" Jack pondered.

"We'll have to track a cart, and see where their new store is," Mingoe suggested.

"I'll follow them. I'm in disguise." Ruby flashed a smile as she pulled her hat even lower. A stout soldier in charge called urgently for help to push a massive water tank towards Cheapside. The whole contraption was so heavy it took thirty people to move it.

Ruby, Mingoe and Jack threw their weight into the combined effort, and the large tank with pumps on either end, was manoeuvred into position. Ruby heard the soldier say, "The hundred houses an hour that burned on Sunday, has become five hundred an hour today. Five hundred families and businesses made homeless. Hour after hour, with no sign of an end."

Ruby left Mingoe and Jack once the tank was operating, raced back to the cathedral, and followed the next cart away. The tea chests were covered with a waxen sheet and she walked directly behind, acutely aware of the two drivers who threatened anyone who clogged their path.

Eventually they surged through Newgate, and just a few hundred metres outside the city walls it felt like a completely different world. She saw people leading a normal life. It was only when she looked back at the smoke climbing from the circle of fire that there was any evidence of the catastrophe.

On the cart trundled to Long Lane in Smithfield where a warehouse door slid open, and it disappeared inside. Ruby loitered in the shadows opposite and watched two more carts arrive. She dropped to the floor and pretended to tie her bootlace. As the door opened she saw the extent of the Packers' Smithfield operation. It was like an Aladdin's cave. At least a dozen men were sorting and stacking stolen items. The door slid shut and she bravely carried on round the building, checking for other exits. She wanted to collect as much information as possible to get them arrested.

Just one back entrance was guarded by two men, completely oblivious to the girl who walked past with her mobcap pulled low over her forehead. Dusk set in and lantern light from inside shone brightly through the high windows. As two more carts arrived, Ruby thought those inside were in for a busy night.

She retraced her steps through the dark streets, towards the huge orange crescent that dominated the skyline. Even Pepys travelled with his sword drawn at night since the fire had started. *Just get back safely*, she said to herself. *Pretend I'm dodging Jasper and Kelvin.* And she knew she could do that easily.

At the fire's front line, Connor and two hundred men commanded by the Duke of York retreated again, as the curtain of flames took another giant step. One by one, he heard officers report the latest news from various locations.

"Your Highness, many churches have succumbed. The stone is no match for this heat, it shatters and splits, then crumbles back to the dust it came from."

"Your Highness, there are attacks on French and Dutch citizens. Your brother's Blue Jackets are patrolling and breaking up mobs intent on violence."

"Your Highness, Samuel Pepys seeks your permission to create a fire break around the Navy Board in Seething Lane. He's recruiting workmen from the king's shipyard and awaits your instructions."

The Duke nodded. "Tell him, yes, with all speed. We want the wind to stop, but if it turns then the Navy Board and the Tower of London will disappear from the earth. Tell him 'fight on', like his gallant servant here who I have stolen for the duration of this battle."

Silhouetted against the surging flames, the Duke shouted to his company. "You have fought for 18 hours. The king and I thank you for your efforts, and we rely on you to rejoin the fight tomorrow."

At his side Connor lost his footing slightly, toppling forwards a little way, still clutching his mighty hooked pole. The Duke steadied him. "Look at this boy, a cook and a musician. Mr Massey here is asleep on his feet, serving the cause. He is but one shining jewel amongst you all."

The Duke called for his cup and fed Connor water. Two hundred voices cheered, and his cheeks flushed afresh at this amazing sign of respect from royalty, who weren't often in the habit of sharing much with servants.

In the cluster of brave fighters, three notable figures stood out. Firstly, the determined and brave, mousey-haired boy, beaming his widest smile at his best friend, who stood beside the king's brother. *How cool was that?* The memory of the Pied Piper and his humiliation in the mall must now be a distant memory for Connor, Freddie hoped.

Secondly, a strong, courageous and clever young girl, who had arrived as the Duke of York began speaking. She had a smile every bit as broad as Freddie's, and tried to catch Connor's eye, but he was so embarrassed by the praise that he stared at his feet.

Ruby caught Freddie's smiling eyes across the crowd, and then they both gasped as between them, a third figure of interest stood shrouded in a huge hood making his face impossible to see. Then he slid back into the shadows, long before the replacement fire fighters arrived and before the Duke had leaped on a horse and rode off for a well-deserved rest – and long before Freddie, Ruby and Connor's exhausted but joyful reunion. Aching and weary, they walked back to Seething Lane having to take a much wider arc around the fire than the day before.

"We'll need proof the Packers are stealing everything. We can't get that wrong. We'll only get one chance," said Freddie.

"Where's the firebreak going to be?" asked Connor.

Freddie stopped dead. "Next to Seething Lane, in Mark Lane… Oh no! Abel Leech's office! We've got to get there and see what's happening!"

Two figures emerged from the shadows outside Pepys's house. Billy Jenks and Percy shuffled nervously from foot to foot, clearly in distress.

"What's wrong Billy?" asked Freddie.

"Our lodgings, is burned and gone. We've lost everything. Well, truth is, me and Ma didn't have much to lose, 'cept the roof. This is her. Queenie she's called, after good Queen Bess."

"Pleased to make your acquaintance," said a voice

from within a pile of clothes. The bundle shifted and a younger-than-expected woman emerged. She was small and pretty, but clearly weak from hunger.

They echoed her greeting, then Freddie said, "Connor can you feed Queenie and the boys, and settle them down in our room."

"We've got to be back with the Duke at 5 am remember," said Connor. "And I've got pies to make before then."

"You make your pies," said Queenie. "I can help. I used to cook in a tavern."

Whilst Connor shepherded the strays to the kitchen, Freddie placed the journal on Pepys's library desk. Then he and Ruby grabbed some bread and cheese and immediately set off to Mark Lane to find out what Leech was up to, or if his office still stood.

"Make sure Pepys sees his journal, and remind him to keep it safe. And get some sleep, Connor," Freddie called to his best friend as they dashed off.

"Yeah, good luck. What if…?" But his friends were already out of earshot.

Chapter 22

"I bet Pepys wants to put the firebreak in Mark Lane to protect his house, not the Navy Board," whispered Ruby, who hadn't taken long to work him out. Mark Lane was one street away and deserted, but the orange sky cast long shadows, like modern street lighting.

Mingoe's hoot came from the alley opposite Leech's house. Ruby and Freddie greeted the two boys.

"Any movement?"

"No. We've been here an hour and nothing," Mingoe replied.

"What shall we do?" Freddie asked.

"Why don't we break in, get Sir Bradley's papers, and then…" The three boys stared at Ruby. It sounded like she did this every day. She frowned. "*What?* It's simple! Here's the best bit. Get Pepys to put the firebreak right *there*." Ruby pointed to the offices of

Howard, Leeming, Farnsworth and Leech.

Her companions were speechless. "Anyone got a better idea?" she asked, and she ran to fetch Percy from Pepys's house. Percy unlocked the large front door in ten seconds, then Mingoe took him back before standing guard.

Jack, Freddie and Ruby crept into the three-storey house where the eerie orange glow filtered through the back windows and lit their way.

They explored the cluttered ground floor full of tea chests. "This must be another Packer hideout," said Ruby. "All the stuff they rescued from Dice Quay."

They climbed the stairs, which creaked and groaned. "What if he's here, asleep?" Freddie whispered. He stepped up the side of the staircase where his steps made less noise and disappeared for a moment, then gave a thumbs up for the others. They copied his method and entered Leech's office at the front of the building.

Ruby sighed. There were dozens of packed shelves, with thousands of loose sheets bound by coloured string and ribbon. It would take days to find one specific set of papers.

"I'll check the top floor," whispered Jack and he slipped away.

"Let's think about this logically," Ruby said.

Freddie nodded. "He'd have these papers in a really safe place because they're so valuable." They concentrated on the green leather-topped desk. Ruby searched the drawers one side, Freddie the other. Both drew a blank.

Jack returned. "Nothing up there. Just bed chambers and cupboards. What exactly are you looking for?" he asked, before taking up watch on the window seat.

"Anything that says Roast, Parsons, Malone, Mingoe, Jack, something like that," Ruby replied.

"If only I could help. When I'm free, someone will teach me to read and write. And I will tell my story in a book. He shifted excitedly on the window seat and dislodged the padded cushion. The trio held their breath as it hit the floor with quite a thud. Nothing in the house moved. "What's that?" said Ruby, pointing.

Underneath was a wooden flap that Ruby lifted to reveal several bundles of papers. Freddie scanned through them while Jack removed the cushions from the other two window seats and opened their hidden chambers. There was nothing in the first two that related to them.

Ruby lifted out the contents of the third hideaway and smiled immediately.

"*What?*" Freddie made a grab for them as Ruby's smile turned into a huge grin and her sapphire eyes flashed with delight.

"Deeds to the Devon farm! Deeds to Alconbury House! And the last Will and Testament of Sir Bradley Fitzhugh Bamburgh Roast!"

"Wow!" gasped Freddie.

"Is it the new will he made just before he died?" asked Jack, scared of the answer Ruby might give.

"Dated August 1665. Yes! Brilliant. That proves Leech was trying to swindle you, by stealing your copy. Look he's even made a fake will, leaving all the farm and everything to him."

The three stared in wonder. "Check again," urged Freddie, unable to believe they had the evidence in their hands.

"No, let's take everything now. Quickly! This is our only chance," said Jack emphatically.

They were euphoric. Mingoe and Jack would be free men, and have a chance of being treated not as slaves and servants, but as proud equals.

They needed something to carry the papers in. Jack returned with a case from upstairs.

"Right, let's…"

An owl hooted.

"Nooooo!" Ruby gasped as she peered out of the window. "It's the shrouded man. He's leading Leech this way. And some of Packer's men are following with carts! What shall we do?"

Freddie jumped to his feet. "Quick! Close these window seats, and let's get upstairs. Maybe they're just coming for the stuff on the ground floor." They tidied quickly and crept up to the top floor. Then they heard the front door open and voices fill the hallway.

"How long ago was this?" said Leech, in his nasal voice. It made Freddie's flesh creep.

"Within the hour," replied the old man.

Loud bangs and crashes signalled that the Packers were taking away more ill-gotten gains, as Leech noisily climbed the stairs.

"Well they're not here now, and I can't see anything missing," he said, as he entered his office. "What would they be after?"

That was all Freddie, Ruby and Jack needed to hear. Leech would go for the window seat and all hell would break loose.

Freddie looked out and tapped Ruby on the shoulder. He pointed at the overhanging roof and gently teased open the window. Warm, smoky air wafted in. Jack went to the door and put as much furniture as possible in front of it. At least they were at the back of the house and Leech's office was at the front, and the men downstairs were making a huge racket moving things.

Ruby's climbing skills were legendary. She grabbed the strong timber border of the roof and pulled herself up. Seconds later she gestured for the case. After placing it safely to one side, she hauled Freddie up. They then had one hand each on Jack's arms, as he easily climbed up beside them.

"It's a flat roof!" Ruby beamed in triumph. Even if that wasn't quite true, it was a very manageable sloping rooftop. They sheltered in the gulley between two peaks. Now they were up they could vanish in either direction. "Which way? And how do we get down?" asked Freddie.

Ruby pulled a face. "Good point, buddy, let's think about that. We could split up and divide the numbers of anyone following, or... One of us could be a decoy – show ourselves and lead them away while the other two escape, or... We could get to the top end of the lane, and where the tallest tree is in the back gardens, jump into it and climb down, or..."

Just then a shriek of rage interrupted Ruby's series of ideas and shattered the night. Leech must have just discovered he'd been robbed. The three fugitives automatically opted for Ruby's last suggestion.

They picked their way up and down the rooftops, holding on to chimneys and pointing out danger spots. They were making good progress, and an owl call sounded away to their right-hand side at street level. Jack replied with his own exotic birdcall and five seconds later the owl hooted again but closer, following their progress along the street. Freddie went to the edge and saw Mingoe dart from shadow to shadow, nearing the junction with Hart Street.

There were three houses to go when they looked back and saw figures emerge onto the roof of Leech's house. Two men went south and two headed in their direction.

Jack made his call three times and Mingoe broke

from cover and shouted to the Packers on the rooftop.

"You're looking in the wrong place, Packers! Here we are!" Mingoe ran round the corner of Hart Street. The gang in the street abandoned their carts and charged after him.

The men on the rooftop stopped, waiting for orders. Freddie, Ruby and Jack scampered silently over the final three crests and in the gully of the last house they sized up the leap they would have to make to the huge tree.

Ruby and Jack were confident they could make it to a sturdy branch about three metres away. Freddie was less sure. This was not his strong point. He was petrified.

"Just go for it, buddy. You can do it," said Ruby. "You'll need a run up, then – *whoosh*. All right?"

Freddie took a deep breath. "If you say so." He wondered how Ruby could be so fearless.

"Jack, you go first, then I'll throw you the case. Let's do this." Ruby seemed completely sure of her plan.

After taking a deep breath, Jack sprinted five paces and launched himself into the air, landing safely in a huge swish of leaves and branches. He sat astride a large horizontal bough, beckoning Freddie on. Ruby threw Jack the case, which he lodged near the trunk. Voices came from the street, as the confused Packers returned, unable to find Mingoe. It didn't sound like they were going to give up, especially as Leech kept shouting, "Find them, you dogs! I need my papers back. It's life and death."

It was now or never for Freddie. He tried to return Ruby's smile. "OK," he gasped. "I can do this." He stood on the edge, visualised his jump and his target. Jack's outstretched arms and the huge bough would be impossible to miss. He measured five steps back and added a sixth for luck.

Ruby gave him the thumbs up and he launched himself forward. With his heart pounding he counted to five and jumped. But he'd forgotten about the extra pace, so launched off the roof sooner than he should have, making him arc out of Jack's reach and plummet down past him and into a cluster of small, sharp branches, which snapped and broke his fall until he dropped to the safety of a bigger bough underneath. It was a disastrous jump, but a triumph in the respect that he was still alive, and he didn't seem to have broken any bones. He tried to smile up at Ruby, who was holding her head in her hands. Then she nimbly landed next to Jack, hardly ruffling a single leaf. *Some people are just good at this kind of stuff,* Freddie thought, as he picked twigs out of his hair.

He led the climb down the huge beech tree into the dark back garden as the confused voices of the Packers echoed through the streets. They hid in the shadows for nearly an hour. Only when the bell at St Olave's struck 2 o'clock, followed almost immediately by an owl call, did they dare break cover. They scrambled over the wall and along to Mark Lane where they showed Sir Bradley's will to Mingoe, who could scarcely believe his eyes.

The two indentured slaves looked at each other through tears of joy, as they realised the dream they'd hoped for was within their grasp once again. The case contained all the legal proof they needed to claim their inheritance, and more importantly, the means to finally start their new lives.

Chapter 23

Tuesday, September 4th, 1666

"It's a terrible day," Pepys said to Connor. "The travelling furnace marches forward house by house, shop by shop, and church by church, and it crushes everyone's spirit. It makes no distinction between squalid back alley hovels and rich merchants' houses, between emporia and palaces. It burns all in its merciless path. God save us!"

They fought the fire alongside the Duke of York, but the battle of Cheapside was lost. The way was clear for the flames to race up to the Guildhall and beyond, and the order was given again to fall back. This time they moved westwards towards St Paul's.

Freddie immediately saw the shrouded figure watching them from the shadows of Sadler's Hall. The three friends stopped and faced their enemy. He simply adjusted his hood further over his head and receded from view.

"He's not even hiding from us now; what does that mean?" Ruby said.

"Why's he always around?" protested Connor, "The other side of the map, in the vortex, Egypt, *everywhere!*"

Freddie pondered. "Let's put ourselves in his shoes. He wants treasures. He wanted the scarab and elixir in Egypt, and the diary and parmesan from my first visit here."

"Wait a second, he tried to hold you back," said Ruby. "I don't think he wants to be here in 1666, I think he wants to be here *later*. Think about it. Who'd want to visit the plague and fire, unless they were crazy?"

"We know he wants the diaries," Connor said. "But Samuel's only halfway through writing those. I bet the hooded bloke wanted to be here when he could steal all five."

"Six, he wrote six volumes, and he stopped in 1670. That's four years from now," said Ruby, recalling what she'd read in the library.

Connor nodded. "Right, so he's probably making the best of it, and hoping to steal the three volumes already written."

Ruby smiled. "And safely on their way to Bethnal Green with Pepys this morning."

Freddie said, "But if we can trap him, by making it look like we've still got those three volumes..."

"And the cheese," added Connor.

"Oh! Yes. And the cheese," smiled Freddie.

This was exciting. They had a plan to work on. They desperately wanted to catch and expose him, but above all, they wanted to stop him from wrecking their adventures.

They were joined by Mingoe and Jack, who'd been helping with the firebreak around Seething Lane. "Leech's office is a pile of bricks. We got those papers just in time," said Mingoe, smiling.

"Fall back to St Paul's!" cried the Duke.

The fire fighters clustered by the cathedral. To Freddie it felt like they were preparing for a last stand as they readied their equipment. The fire was approaching fast, and only the north side provided a clear escape route. The Packers had long since vanished, but they'd locked the crypt doors on both sides to protect their goods.

There was nervous conversation all around them. "I got a golden guinea from the king himself this morning, look," said a red-faced man. His friend nodded. "They say the madhouse fell last night and bewildered souls roam the streets in their night dresses, not knowing if they're in heaven or hell."

A loud voice proclaimed, "I helped to save £10,000 in gold coins from the flames at Sir Richard Browne's house. Guess what he gave the six of us that helped?"

"What?"

"Four pounds! Between us! I wish I'd let his fortune melt with his mansion." There was laughter and agreement in equal measure.

Another voice cut through. "As the Exchange burned, the statues of the kings and queens toppled one after the other into the ashes." A silence fell after that. Freddie knew the stories weren't exaggerated. The truth was all too real.

Then it was upon them. The brave collection of butchers, bakers and candlestick makers faced the 30-metre flames on the south side of the cathedral. The shops and houses Freddie had seen when he first arrived burned in front of his eyes. The ferocious heat forced everyone back to the cathedral wall.

Suddenly a cry sounded from their right, "Look!" Everyone turned to see a tiny fan of flames half-way up the tinder-dry scaffolding. By the time five men had climbed with buckets, the blaze had stretched and spread left and right. Freddie knew that the Great Fire of London had started on its most famous prize.

At close on 8 o'clock in the evening on Tuesday, the 4th September 1666, the wooden latticework that surrounded the outside of the building became an overcoat of fire. It spread upwards so quickly, nothing could be done to stop it. More planks and beams ready for the restoration work were stored on the roof.

When these caught alight, a raging inferno melted the lead they stood on, and in turn, the huge wooden ceiling underneath. The roof of the mighty building crashed to the ground over fifty metres below. Then the walls began to buckle and crumble, showering the cathedral floor with falling masonry, shattering the patterned marble, allowing molten lead and burning crossbeams to fall through and feast on the packed crypt full of books and valuables.

Everyone ran round to the north side of the building, and most kept on running. With the collapse of St Paul's, it felt like London was lost.

A small, loyal group gathered around the Duke and watched as the massive edifice crumbled. He set off north to set up another firebreak. The five friends stared for one last time at the devastation, and were about to follow when Freddie saw a hand waving from a crack in the stonework on the crypt stairway. One tiny hand, desperately pleading for rescue.

"Look!" He pointed. Without thinking, he moved forward with Mingoe, Jack, Ruby and Connor at his side.

They all looked at each other in desperation. 'What shall we do?" Ruby asked.

"Bring water buckets and let's try to smash the door down," Freddie yelled. Mingoe and Jack used an abandoned demolition spike, and after six good thumps the door around the lock splintered and gave way. They pulled it open and released thick black smoke, which poured out of the deadly basement. Freddie held his nose and felt round to his right to where the hand had shown through the crack. Ruby shouted through the hole, "Help's coming. Wave so we know you're still alive."

A small grubby hand thrust its way through the gap and Ruby stroked it and shouted, "Feel around you. My friend has come to get you out. See if you can grab him." The tiny hand disappeared again and a terrible wait ensued. Twice Jack charged into the basement, cleared debris and tried to help but came out empty-handed. Mingoe tore off his shirt-sleeves and soaked them in water. Wrapping one round his face and carrying the other, he entered, and 20 seconds later he emerged coughing and spluttering, but leading Freddie who had the other soaked sleeve clasped over a small boy's mouth.

The three collapsed on the ground and Connor splashed water over them while they caught their breath. A massive crash of masonry shattered the cathedral floor just along from the staircase, and the dense smoke that had come out of the door found a more convenient escape route through the huge new hole.

"Are you all right?" Ruby asked the gasping boy who rolled over onto his back. Freddie was amazed as the boy's green eyes shot open. "There's twenty of us. The

Packers locked us in to guard the sparkle."

Freddie searched his friends' faces. "What can we do?" he shouted.

"We need a rope so we can lead them out," cried Ruby, looking around. "We can run in, grab the children and when we tug on the rope, pull them out." Jack found a coil of rope by a deserted water tank. They tied it to their waists and copied Mingoe. They tore off their shirtsleeves and doused them in water before tying one around their heads and carrying the other for a child.

Jack led the way in. At least the dense black smoke had cleared a little. Ruby was tied on the rope next, and she entered leaving Mingoe by the door to pull the rope when needed. Freddie and Connor tried to protect Mingoe from falling debris, but they knew that if a large piece of stonework fell, they'd all be dead.

The rope was tugged and Mingoe pulled first Ruby and then Jack out of the building. Between them were two small boys who were close to collapse. Freddie and Connor helped them away.

"Get your breath back," Mingoe shouted to Ruby above the cacophony around them.

"Where are the children?" Freddie asked the green-eyed boy.

He pointed to the right, and in a smoke ravaged voice said, "There, down a few steps on that side."

"Look after them and get more water," Freddie

said to the boy. Then he and Connor relayed the position of the children. Jack and Ruby were still wiping their streaming eyes, but ready for another attempt. Dipping the sleeves in water, they took huge breaths, but suddenly Ruby felt the rope go taut. They looked round and saw Connor with the loose end of the rope tied round his waist disappear through the door with one of his own sleeves wrapped around his nose. He plunged into the chaos of fear and flame.

Ruby followed, then Jack. As the seconds ticked by, a steady stream of abandoned children inched their way along the rope from Connor to Ruby to Jack, and to freedom. Bursting for fresh air, one by one, the collection of motley vagrants, pickpockets and cut purses spilled out to the relative safety of the square.

"Count them," Mingoe shouted to Freddie.

"Eleven, no twelve. Twelve so far."

Jack and Ruby emerged moments later with five more. But the rope was severed between Ruby and Connor. She held the smouldering end where a burning beam had fallen and cut the lifeline.

Freddie sprang into action as Jack and Ruby recovered. He grabbed her spare sleeve, dipped it in water, and thrust himself into the danger.

Once inside, he could see nothing. The smoke naturally went high so he crouched and he felt his way down five steps. That was better. Now he could see the dancing lights of a million flames away to his left.

But the terrible memories of the burning monastery at Thyangboche flooded his brain and he completely froze. He couldn't move in any direction.

What seemed like an eternity passed and suddenly Ruby was at his side, pulling him back. "Quick, Freddie, you can't help, you're in the way. Let me get Connor." She forced him back towards the door, then took a huge breath and re-entered.

Ruby raced to the fallen beam, which illuminated the entire space. But at the same time it set light to the tea chests either side of the narrow walkway. If she was to rescue Connor and the remaining children, it had to be now. She took a step towards the beam, hoping she could jump over it. But some of the stone from the cathedral above collapsed, and a small sheet of marble flooring glanced her side, knocking her over, and pinning her leg to the ground. It was so heavy she couldn't lift it. However hard she struggled, it just wouldn't move.

The collapsed flooring had snuffed out a lot of the fire around her, but out of the corner of her eye she watched a thick trickle of molten lead trying to find the quickest route into the bowels of the cathedral. It was like watching lava flow. It started a new pillar of flame two metres to her right. The scalding metal was heading straight for Ruby.

Then Mingoe and Jack arrived at her side. On the third attempt they lifted the marble slab away from her trapped leg. Ruby jumped sideways from the molten lead, which would have engulfed her in another ten seconds.

A revitalised Freddie rushed back in with fresh watered sleeves which the children had donated. They were about to launch themselves in Connor's direction, when something magical happened.

Out of the smoke and flames, with scalding debris and molten lead splashing all around, Connor led a line of three small waifs, all with their arms on the shoulder in front. The large dishevelled boy had a scarf around his nose, and his smoke-stung eyes could just see the escape route ahead. But quite incredibly, in his mouth was a recorder, and he was playing the Pied Piper's tune as if leading the rats away from Hamelin. It was at once the strangest and most wonderful thing Freddie thought he had ever seen or heard.

They seemed indestructible, impervious to the chaos around them. As flames and falling masonry peppered the sides of their escape route, the small boys had their eyes on the ground, picking a safe route for their shuffling feet. When they reached the fallen beam, Mingoe, Jack and Freddie launched the marble slab, crumpling the barrier in two, giving Connor and his three blind mice a clear path.

Ruby thrust wet sleeves at the boys who clutched them to their scalded faces, and with Connor leading the way, the bedraggled band emerged into the fresh air of Paternoster Square. They collapsed in a doorway 50 metres from the cascading masonry that pelted the ground. Bizarrely, Connor carried on playing until the end of the song. And the silence that followed was one of wonder.

The moment was broken by Freddie. He asked the green-eyed boy, "Are all your friends safe?" The same green-eyed boy who'd tried to rob him, who'd been sent into plague houses, who'd dodged the deadly disease, who'd marched with the survivors, who'd spotted Ruby's arrival, and who'd now been rescued metres from where he'd attacked Freddie in the first place, checked his team.

"Yes they're all here. Thank you, mister. I thought we was going to cook. I know you, don't I?" he added. Freddie smiled, and as the bedraggled band moved away from the disaster, he told the boy, whose name was Knibbs, all about their complicated history.

Then Ruby stopped still. "What's different?" she said in a worried voice. "Something's changed." A nearby church bell sounded 11 times.

"It's the wind," said Freddie in a worried whisper, "It's blowing the other way. It's blowing to the east. Towards the Tower! That means the fire's going to turn."

Chapter 24

Mingoe and Jack led them to Seething Lane over cobbles that were hot underfoot. They passed the departing shipyard workers, who with the aid of gunpowder and grappling hooks had finished creating the firebreak on Mark Lane. They were all delighted to see the ruins of Abel Leech's office. It was a proper and fitting punishment for his treachery.

Mingoe stumbled over a box. It had nine fuses left inside. The five divided them between themselves. "How do they work?" asked Connor.

"You put them in the top of a barrel of gunpowder and light the end. Then you run. The fuse burns to the count of fifteen." Mingoe illustrated the explosion with his hands.

"Wow," said Connor, hoping he got to use one.

Once back home, they helped Pepys's wife onto a

cart along with his fortune of £2,350. With the fire fast approaching, away she rode with Hewer and the staff to Woolwich and to safety.

Pepys told Freddie he was convinced his house would burn now the wind had turned. "And the Tower as well. It's stacked with gunpowder and all the gold, silver and jewels the London goldsmiths moved there for safekeeping. The Navy are transferring it again onto ships. We must dig a hole in the gardens to bury what can't be carried."

They took turns creating a large pit. Pepys handed down dozens of bottles of claret wine and watched the others struggle with his enormous Parmesan cheese, which was then covered with wood.

Freddie whispered to Ruby and Connor, "Keep watch for the shrouded man." He produced three ledgers, bound similarly to Pepys's journals. Showing them off like sports trophies, he placed them in the ground under the wooden board.

Ruby grinned. "Brilliant, buddy. The trap is set!"

Pepys moved back to the house, probably wondering why Freddie wanted to save Navy records about salted fish stocks, ships' biscuits, and the renewal dates for mainsails. He then followed Elizabeth to Woolwich, and Freddie was left with instructions to save Seething Lane from the fire. "Yes, sir! We'll try."

After Connor had fed them, Queenie led the homeless waifs to the safety of Whittington Palace.

Looking out of the window by the front door, Ruby whispered to herself, "Someone's watching us. I can feel it." Then she joined Freddie in the kitchen where Connor was already snoring in the corner.

"One of us has to stay awake," she said.

"They'll attack just before dawn, I reckon," said Freddie. "I'll take first watch, and wake you in two hours." St Olave's had just struck 3 o'clock, and Ruby was asleep in an instant. Despite every attempt not to succumb, even pacing the house on patrol, Freddie eventually sat down on the stairs overlooking the back garden, but drifted off ten minutes later. It had been that sort of day.

Their rest didn't last long. Almost immediately an owl hooted urgently outside. Freddie jumped up, calling down to the others. From the window he could clearly see shapes digging at the hole.

"There's ten of them out front as well," said Ruby. "With a cart."

The plan was that as soon as the Packers attacked, both Mingoe and Jack, on guard next door, were to fetch either the King's Troop, the Blue Jackets, or the sailors from Tower Wharf.

Connor went upstairs where he could see out of windows front and back. He froze as he saw one of the Packers pick the lock and enter Sir William Batten's house with Leech. *The case! I bet that's what they want,* Connor thought. *This is a disaster!* And sure enough, within a minute Leech emerged, clutching his prize. They had to get it back or Mingoe and Jack would be slaves for another thirty five years.

Meanwhile, in the back garden the men were about to lift the wooden board off the cheese. The three books were held aloft and passed to Bob Packer, who laughed as he threw aside the bottle of Pepys's claret he was drinking. "What a lot of fuss over words," he scoffed, not whispering anymore, knowing their mission was almost complete. Connor raced downstairs and told the terrible news of the case.

"No!" Ruby said.

Freddie felt clearheaded and strode over to the front window. "The cheese is unimportant, and the books are fakes, they're just the trap. But we must get the case. Forget everything else." He saw Leech reward the thug, then stand next to the shrouded figure who was supervising the loading of the Parmesan.

The cluster of men drifted away, leaving Bob, who ordered two others to pull the cart. He held out the three books, and the shrouded man danced on the spot, rubbing his hands excitedly.

"Ready?" whispered Freddie. His two friends nodded with different amounts of confidence.

"Let's go!" He flung open the door and raced towards Leech. Ruby overtook him and with a powerful rugby tackle flattened the oily lawyer. Freddie swooped and picked up the case and dragged Ruby back to her feet.

Several metres behind them, Connor, slammed into the shrouded figure, who crumpled against the cart and practically handed the books over before sagging to the floor.

Bob Packer was the far side of the cart and got tangled with the others who all made a move at the same time. These few vital seconds gave the large, lumbering boy time to get some speed up, and he followed Freddie and Ruby towards Whittington Palace.

Bob who shouted after his men, "Get them! I need that case and those books. It's a guinea to the man that returns either one." He limped on behind, leaving the extraordinary sight of a 40-kilogram cheese on a cart outside Pepys's house.

Connor was eating up the metres, striding out like a rugby player, pursued by the pack of 17th-century cutthroats.

As they reached the palace Freddie thrust the case and books at Ruby. "Quick, upstairs! We'll hold them off."

"Good luck." She was already at the top of the first staircase.

"Make a barricade here," said Connor, pulling over an old wardrobe and grabbing one end of a table. Freddie yelled to Queenie and the waifs, "Hide! The Packers are coming." After the boys helped with the barricade, they scuttled into the shadows, as they'd been doing all their lives. Freddie grabbed the two pikes from an armoury display above the fireplace and vaulted behind the table, which was wedged at the bottom of the staircase.

Lowering the lethally sharp weapons onto the rim of the table coincided with the arrival of the first Packers. They hesitated, not wanting to lose a hand trying to pull the pikes away. Freddie and Connor jerked and prodded in the direction of anyone who made a move, giving Ruby more time to escape. The gang formed an attacking semicircle. Soon, two were out of action with badly cut wrists. Bob hobbled to the centre and was about to speak when Freddie shouted, "Go, Connor, go!" Connor took the stairs two at a time.

Freddie used both pikestaffs to keep the mob at bay, sweeping back and forth.

"Take him, one of you! He's just a boy!" Bob shouted. Several men lurched forward at once. Freddie caught two of them with his left-hand weapon, but the right was grabbed and pulled by a ferocious bearded man who screamed at Freddie. Freddie screamed back, and shoved the pike with all his might, hurting the man badly. He collapsed backwards into the mob.

Freddie ran upstairs. He caught Connor on the second landing, who'd spotted more furniture for a barricade. They heard the pounding feet following them up. Freddie pulled Connor away. "Help Ruby upstairs in the gallery," he whispered.

As the first four men turned the corner and started towards Freddie, he pushed the collection of heavy wooden objects with all his might. They crashed down the staircase, flattening the first pursuers and a few of those directly behind. He was buying valuable time. Surely Mingoe and Jack would bring help soon. Ruby shouted down, "Come on, Freddie!"

The remaining fit men climbed over both the furniture and their fallen colleagues and moved on up cautiously. Others were hauled to their feet by Bob, who followed.

Connor and Ruby reached the long gallery at the very top of the palace, with its huge windows revealing an eerie orange glow and casting long shadows. As they walked backwards across the sagging floor, Connor realised that Freddie hadn't followed them up.

Ruby handed the books to him and whispered, "Remember, Connor, we can afford to lose the books… But not the case. If all else fails, I'll smash a window and throw the case out. Are you with me, buddy?"

"Yes," Connor replied, struggling to control his fear. There was still no Freddie. They reached the table by the fireplace with their escape doors either side and tried the handles.

"Mine's locked," said Connor.

"Try it again."

"I have. It won't move."

Ruby cursed. "Mine's stuck as well. We're trapped."

The first of the pursuing gang entered the room.

"Come over here," Ruby whispered out of the side of her mouth, never taking her eyes off the men. "You work on my lock." Connor tried to loosen the handle, but it wouldn't budge.

Twelve gang members edged towards them. There were seven fit men, and five walking wounded. Loitering in the background were the shrouded man and Leech. Then strutting like an injured prize fighter across the creaking floor, Bob Packer walked to the middle of the room. That made a total of 15 against Ruby and Connor.

"So, it comes to this. Yer final throw of the dice hasn't gone well, has it?" Bob smirked. "It looks like those doors is locked. All we've got to do is walk up and take what's ours."

"They're not yours," said Ruby. "They belong to other people, and it's our job to return them safely."

"Ha! Well I can assure you those books are going to a lovely home, and this here Leech says the papers are legally his."

"He's lying. They both are. You're just not clever enough to understand."

"Not clever? I know fifteen beats three!"

"You're a thug and a bully."

Bob smirked. "Why, thank you! What a compliment." His cronies laughed. "So, Bluey, you've still not learned to shut up. I shall enjoy every penny piece of the money I get for you. Now get the fat boy to bring me the books, and then the case. But books first. My original employer is impatient. Move it!"

Neither moved. Bob gestured to his men. The old wooden floor creaked under the combined weight of the gang.

Ruby whispered to Connor, "Go halfway really slowly. Buy as much time as you can. Then throw the books high in the air so they'll have to scramble for them. OK?"

Connor shuffled slowly into the room. Every step he took was accompanied by creaking wood, but at least he'd stopped the advance of the Packers, who gathered in the middle waiting for the handover.

"That's a good boy," proclaimed Bob, holding something behind his back.

"Careful, Connor, he's armed," shouted Ruby.

"Too late now, Bluey, your fat friend's in for it." The gang laughed. "I love the way big ones squeal."

Connor was shaking with fear. He halted his advance across the floor. Bob kept walking, and produced the cudgel. Ruby felt the door handle turning from the other side.

"Lesson one, fat boy..." Bob snarled, but he had no time to say anything else as Connor launched the books up into the air with all his might. They arced up, and fifteen pairs of eyes followed their flight, whilst thirty hands made to catch them before they hit the floor. At the same time, the door behind Ruby shot open and Freddie shouted, "Connor, run. Quick!"

As Connor turned and ran, the gang pounced on the books, eager for the guinea reward. "Get them! Get the case!" Packer shouted. Freddie launched a missile at Bob, whose surprised expression betrayed his fear. And he was right to be afraid.

A fizzing fuse attached to a small casket, spun through the air towards the vile man. Chaos ensued as the men tried to evade the explosive. Bob caught the box and made to throw it back, when the deafening sound of splitting wood filled the air as the rotten planks of the gallery floor finally gave way under their weight. Dust, debris and splinters remained where a second before the gang had all stood. The men's screams joined the elongated boom of falling flooring as they tumbled through the gaping hole and thudded into the room below, where the floor also gave way under the sudden onslaught of a dozen men and tons of wooden beams.

But Bob wasn't finished. He'd dropped his cudgel and caught the box with the lighted fuse. He clung to the side of the hole with his spare arm and launched the lighted box back at the three friends clustered in the doorway.

Freddie caught it as Ruby and Connor flung themselves to the floor. He removed the fuse, trod on it, and extinguished the flame. Then he opened the box to reveal… Nothing! The edges of the hole under Bob's arms started splintering, and the three friends slid the heavy table from in front of the fireplace towards the floundering man. The extra weight was too much and a screaming Bob Packer followed his hateful gang down two storeys to land in a heap of broken table and bones.

Clustered together, Freddie, Ruby and Connor shook with relief. Across the gallery, two feeble figures snarled at them before scuttling away down the stairs. The Packers were destroyed and their broken bodies lay groaning in a sorry pile.

The waifs of St Paul's emerged from the shadows with nets and ropes and bound them where they lay, to take a just and sweet revenge for being left to die in the burning cathedral.

Chapter 25

Freddie, Connor and Ruby ran down the back staircase and found Queenie hitting reviving gang members on the head with a large saucepan lid. Soon they were all safely gagged and bound, including a furious Bob Packer who had two broken legs and a nasty bruise on his forehead, not from the fall, but from Queenie.

"I enjoyed that last one especially," she said smiling. Suddenly the first floor room was full of the Blue Jackets led by Colonel De Vere, flanked by Mingoe and Jack. They were overwhelmed with joy to get their case back. Jack cradled it like a newborn baby, and Ruby spilled all her information about the Packers' warehouse in Long Lane to De Vere. "Thank you. All of you," said the Colonel. "The people of this city owe you so much. We'll make sure these brutes get the justice they deserve. Mr Malone, we meet again."

Freddie nodded and smiled as the soldiers dragged the villains away to a waiting cart.

Ruby turned to Mingoe. "Before anything else happens, take the papers to safety. We'll tidy up here," she said.

"Don't worry they won't leave our hands," said Jack, as they carried their future freedom away.

Billy Jenks and Percy stepped forward and handed over three battered books. Freddie didn't have the heart to tell them they were worthless.

"Thank you, Billy."

"It was Percy who spotted them. Bob landed right on them as he came through the ceiling. Broke his fall they did. All those words cushioned his backside." The small boys laughed.

Knibbs stood with one foot on Bob's chest, with his arms in the air like a wrestling champion at Bartholomew Fair. Bob writhed with anger, but there was nothing he could do to stop them celebrating. They all took their turn, and it only finished when Bob was grabbed by his two broken legs and carried off. Even through the tight gag, it was a scream that most of London probably heard.

"*The cheese!*" Freddie suddenly shouted. "Connor, help Queenie settle the waifs, and Ruby and I will rescue Samuel's precious Parmesan." Laughing at the thought of it, the triumphant pair turned the corner by St Olave's Church.

"Well my doves, here's a change of fortune, wouldn't you say?" A cloud of pipe smoke swirled out of the shadows, and Old Ma Packer spat a long drizzle into the churchyard grass. In front of her, Mingoe and Jack were tied to the metal railings with their embroidered 'kerchiefs stuffed in their mouths. Next to them stood toothless Aggie with a knife at Mingoe's throat, and a hideous smile across her face.

Old Ma was right. This *did* change things. Leech stepped forwards, reunited with his case, followed by the shrouded man.

Old Ma started again. "Now, Irish, you've cost me a lot of money, and I've quite run out of patience. This gentleman, the one that don't like to be seen, he's willing to double what he offered me for them books. One hundred pounds he's paying, so you'd have to cough up two hundred to stop me. I know you can't pay that, so hand them over nice and calm, and then these two," – she indicated Mingoe and Jack – "will be spared. If you don't, Aggie will use her bluntest chiv on your friends and that won't be nice to watch. Truth be told, Aggie don't want you to hand over the books, she's keen to see if these dark ones have red blood like ours. Ain't I a terrible mother, bringing up my children to behave like that?" Old Ma trailed off with a hollow laugh.

Freddie cleared his throat. "Here's the deal. You can have the books for nothing."

"That's better, Irish. I knew you'd see sense," she began.

"I haven't finished. In exchange for the case."

"What?" exclaimed Leech.

"Yes, do it! Do it!" whispered the shrouded man, whose chin emerged slightly from his hood. "Just get me the books."

"Well now, what's this?" The old woman clenched her pipe between her teeth and puffed. "I get the books for nothing, and I sell them to the shy one, but I take the case from this here lawyer and give it to you? Am I reading this right?"

"Quite right," said Ruby, with a nod.

"Ah! Bluey, I couldn't part with such a precious commodity for so little reward."

Leech quietened, realising Old Ma wasn't going to accept that deal. "How about I get the books, which I sell to the shy man, and in exchange for this here very, *very* valuable case, young Bluey steps over to my side in return. She's a prize just about equal to a case full of important papers."

Mingoe and Jack both shook their heads as forcefully as they could, until Aggie threatened them again.

Freddie moved in front of Ruby, but she pushed past him. "All right. It's worth it. Someone has to right the wrongs that have been done to them, and if that has to be me, then here I am."

"No, Ruby," said Freddie. "Please!"

"Clever girl. My Bluey. I knew you was valuable." Old Ma thought about things and then nodded. "So on my count of three, the books go to the shy man, Aggie cuts these boys free, Bluey steps to my side, and the case goes to young Irish. Have I missed anything out?"

"Yes!" screamed Leech, they're my papers. You're not giving them away to anyone." He ran for the safety of the church, but a silver flash spun through the air and pinned his coat sleeve to the door.

Then, from out of the darkness, Connor launched a lighted fuse stuck firmly in a ball of horse manure. He threw it at Aggie as she was reaching down for the knife that she kept in her boot. Ruby and Connor pushed her over. Freddie grabbed the knife and released Jack, who took over and cut Mingoe's bonds. Then he raced and got the case whilst Freddie and Jack threw themselves at Old Ma. They tied her hands behind a stout tree trunk amongst the plague graves.

Still pinned to the church door, Leech was screaming revenge. They bound his legs, and after removing the knife, his hands as well. Aggie was no match for Connor, who proved to be an immovable object when sitting on her back. He wiped his manure-covered hands on her long dress, whilst Ruby took great pleasure in tying her securely.

It couldn't have worked out any better. Except the shrouded man was gone. And so, unsurprisingly, were the books.

Apart from missing out on exposing their enemy, it was the best possible outcome. After piling their prisoners on the pavement to await the King's Troop, the five friends celebrated their victory watching the sun rise over The Tower of London, bathing them all in its light.

As they guarded their prisoners, they saw Pepys hurrying up from the river. He kept looking over his shoulder and nearly tripped twice. Not far behind him came a large group of uniformed sailors.

"Quick, Fred, save me. Sailors from the good ship *Assurance* demand their wages. They promise they'll rob me if I don't pay. Save me, boy. Talk to 'em. Protect your lord and master." Pepys was twittering like a frightened mouse. He took shelter behind Freddie, but then moved swiftly to the larger barrier of Connor.

About 40 sailors came to a halt. A small, red-haired man with a permanent smile said, "We've no argument with you, friends. You're his servants, I suppose. God help you."

"Why are you chasing him?" asked Freddie.

"Because, we've been at sea two years, and not been paid. Not only that, many of us were taken against our will to fight the Dutch. None of us want to go to war with anyone. But the king commands, and we were taken. We've all left families behind who don't know if we live or not. So once again, friend, I say, step aside, this Pepys will pay us either with Navy money or his own, it makes no difference to us." The men behind him echoed agreement.

Pepys stuttered, "But the Navy Board is evacuated. All valuables have been taken. Look, the fire's three streets away. Search the building, it's empty." He shrank back behind Connor.

"My... You're a weasel man aren't you?" said the spokesman. "While you sat at your fancy feasts, supping on port wine and best beef, we was riding those deadly seas drinking vile water and eating worm castle biscuits which near killed us all. This country owes us for that, and this country will pay. And as you represent this country, you will pay its debt. Then you can reclaim your spending from the king, next time you're at table with him."

"I can't let you hurt my master," said Freddie. "And 40 against one isn't fair, no matter how much wrong you've been done, so I have an idea. How much are you owed?"

"A lot, my friend. We have a ledger here, all itemised, services listed and wages outstanding. It comes to...?" A young man stepped forward and opened a pocket book. "Three hundred and ninety nine pounds, ten shillings, and sixpence."

He showed the page to Pepys.

"Where can I possibly conjure that from? I'm no magician. Money doesn't—"

For the first time the smile disappeared from the

face of the small man, making his words all the more powerful. "Then you're our hostage until it's paid. You'll be treated as we were, and fed as we were, and put to work as we were. The choice is yours."

"I think I can help," said Freddie. "These three prisoners have done the whole of London wrong. I've no doubt they carry money which could go towards the debt."

Ma, Aggie and Leech were roughly searched by some of the sailors, and three purses were extracted. The contents were quickly counted by the ledger man, who pronounced, "Nearly one hundred pounds give or take a shilling or two. It's a start but you fall a long way short."

Freddie smiled and turned to Pepys. "Are you wearing your loose breeches today, sir?" he asked.

"My what? Are you touched with madness, Fred? My loose bree—"

"Yes, sir, the breeches which need that strong belt you showed me." Freddie's eyes danced with devilment.

"My belt. Why my belt is… You mean my *belt* belt?" queried Pepys.

"Yes, sir, your *belt* belt."

"But my breeches will fall down without my *belt* belt."

"You can have the belt back, sir. It's the contents these fine men want," said Freddie, proud of his solution.

Two sailors lifted Pepys up by the arms and another removed the belt from his waist, revealing compartment after compartment of gold coins.

"No, no! That's mine," Pepys pleaded, holding up his falling trousers.

"We'll give you an itemised receipt, to claim back your outlay," said the spokesman, his smile twice as big as before.

"Three hundred," said the ledger man, tearing a signed page from his log.

Pepys looked at the paper and accepted his now-empty belt back with an ungrateful 'harrumph'. "I need your name and address, to call you as witness."

"Of course, very prudent of you," said the small smiling man. "It's Jenks. Johnny Jenks."

Moments later, Queenie, Billy and Johnny Jenks stood hugging each other in a tight knot, after Ruby had fetched them from Whittington Palace, saying, "I've got a surprise." The Jenks family had fallen into each other's arms in the middle of Seething Lane.

Billy's smile was every bit as big as his dad's.

Freddie explained everything to Pepys as he helped him with his belt. "At least you'll be able to walk a lot quicker now that weight's gone," said Freddie, risking a clip round the ear. The truth was Freddie felt confident, he felt like things were resolving, and as soon as the fire was under control it would be time to leave. There was just one more thing he needed to be absolutely certain of.

"Sir, there's one favour I'd ask."

"What? Not a pay rise. I won't hear of it."

"No, sir, not a pay rise. We have papers from the estate of Sir Bradley Roast. I'd like you to oversee that his wishes are carried out, and that Mingoe and Jack can buy out their indentures and become free men, and both inherit a third each of the estate. The other third I would like you to transfer from my name and replace it with Johnny, Queenie and Billy Jenks, as they deserve a new start more than I do."

Pepys shuffled the papers that Mingoe presented to him. He stared in wonder at the documents and read, and re-read certain sections, before looking up and pronouncing, "It would be an honour to see these wishes carried out. What a wonderful turn of events. This morning I stood on All Hallows Tower surveying the desolation, and I thought all hope lost, but you show me these simple wishes, and the world doesn't seem such a terrible place.

"Mr Jack and Mr Min— err, sorry, Mr Kwanza, you'll be welcome to share a bottle or two of my best claret, and dine at my table at the earliest opportunity. That is, if Mr Packer has left me any claret to drink!"

Chapter 26

Freddie smiled, as by mid-morning on Wednesday, 5th September, Leech, Aggie and Old Ma Packer had been collected by the Watch and taken for trial near Moor Fields, but not until Mingoe had used Aggie's knife and cut a tiny nick in his thumb. A single blob of bright red blood stood out. He showed it to the girl and smiled, before wiping it on her sleeve as a permanent reminder. He held her gaze for a very long time as his smile faded to a cold stare.

Whilst the Watch loaded them on a cart, Pepys noted, "They will pass through the refugee camps, housing not only victims of the fire, but also all the families they robbed during the plague and for decades before." At least, thought Freddie, their empire had now crumbled thanks to the efforts of a lot of brave people, and their punishment awaited.

Some waifs were sent in search of the shrouded man, but drew a blank. Though Knibbs did bring back news. "The fire's dying out at last, and the king's gone to Hampton Court. People are charging tuppence for a penny loaf, and a landlord said, 'Fifty thousand Dutchies are marching on London'." Pepys seemed *most* upset at the price of bread.

A Navy messenger arrived just after noon to say the fire had been halted at Holborn in the west, and then at Pie Corner near Newgate. That left the last outbreak at Bishopsgate, but even that was nearly finished.

The small band wandered the short distance to Tower Street, and at the corner of Mark Lane, Ruby observed just how close the flames had come. One street stood between them and destruction. In front, as far as she could see, was a wasteland.

Pepys repeated what he'd said on All Hallows Tower, where the fire had actually lapped its front door. "This was the saddest sight of desolation that I ever saw."

Connor realised that the only things that stood more than five metres off the ground were the shattered stumps of church towers. Smoke rose from where flames had feasted. He saw occasional flares burst out in vibrant colour, amidst the grey ash and charred wood that was strewn at strange angles like a ravaged forest.

A meowing sounded from a nearby ruin. Shakily, a

scalded cat jumped down from inside a stone chimney and wobbled unsteadily towards them. All its fur was gone but it was alive, and it took little persuasion to follow Ruby back for some food. To have survived the plague cull *and* the fire was some feat.

"What's going to happen to the children?" Freddie asked Pepys on the walk.

"I've been thinking about them, and I believe the headmaster of Westminster School might help. I shall persuade some of my wealthy friends to provide scholarships, and give them a chance of a new life, as you've done for the Jenks boy. I might even sponsor one or two myself, to thank God for sparing my home."

"Thank you, sir," said Freddie. "That would be amazing."

"But tell me, Fred, why are you giving up your share? You could live like a king."

Freddie had known Pepys would ask this. "I must return to Ireland. I haven't been entirely truthful, I'm from a very wealthy family who can look after me. I've had a wonderful time in London but actually, it's a bit quiet and boring. I've only witnessed the plague, a kidnapping, a year at sea on the *Hispaniola*, and then the fire. *Nothing ever happens here!* I'm going back home for some excitement."

Pepys roared with laughter. "The wit of the Irish! I will miss you, Fred." Then he said, "And your friends?"

"Ruby and Connor are coming with me."

"No! Not Connor. Please? What shall I eat? What music will I make without him?

"You'll find someone, sir, I'm sure you will."

Pepys shook his head. "Not with his skills and sensitivity. He'll go far, mark my words."

Reaching home, Pepys read a message just received from the Navy Board. "Eighty-seven churches, six chapels and St Paul's. The Customhouse, the Royal Exchange, four prisons, and the Guildhall gutted. They say over thirteen thousand dwellings are gone, and maybe eighty thousand are homeless." He stared out of his library window. "Four days during which a fifth of London has been destroyed."

Pepys called Mingoe, Jack and Johnny Jenks for a meeting, and Freddie knew it was time to get going. As exciting as the 17th century was, Christmas was calling them home.

All their friends were very upset when Freddie explained that they were returning to Ireland.

"We ain't never gonna to forget any of you," said Billy Jenks in his rasping voice, before making to wipe his nose with his sleeve.

Queenie stopped him. "It's not *ain't*, Billy, it's *are not*," she said. "Ain't that right, Freddie?" Even Queenie giggled at her mistake.

"Percy and his mum are coming to live with us in Devon on Sir Bradley's farm," said Johnny Jenks. "Samuel's sorting it all out."

"There's pigs, 'n cows, 'n sheepsies, *ain't* there, Ma?"

"Oh! I give up," said Queenie ruffling Billy's hair.

"And Mingoe and me are going to start up Sir Michael Povey's Emporium again," said Jack with wonder. "Mr Pepys has written to Boggy to settle the matter."

The two former slaves shook their heads in disbelief and Mingoe added, "We will work harder than anyone, and open shops in every port and become proper gentlemen."

"You always were proper gentlemen," said Freddie. "And the best friends a lost boy in a plague city could ever wish for."

"Aren't you forgetting something?" Ruby said. "Your collars!" Jack carefully unclipped the silver and brass collar containing his indenture, and stared at Sir William Penn's coat of arms. He shone the dulled metal on his coat, wiping away four days of dirt.

"I shall ask to purchase this shackle, to remind me of my journey, and that of my father, and my father's father."

Mingoe did the same, and the two former slaves stared at each other with fiercely determined expressions, remembering the history of their struggle, and fuelling the belief in their futures.

A pall of smoke still rose from the packed crypt of St Paul's. Much of the stock continued to burn, and in places the stonework and cobbles were still glowing red.

The three friends stood and looked at the buried entrance to the crypt and Connor touched his recorder, which had become a fixture in his belt, almost like a sword.

All around the cathedral the collapsed masonry formed huge piles. The lead had solidified, and now sat like grey icing on a stone cake. As they approached the front, even the mighty bells had melted, and a pool of liquid metal still steamed and fizzed.

Freddie froze in panic.

"What's wrong?" asked Ruby.

"The portal!" Freddie pointed. "It's under that lot." A vast heap of rubble covered their escape route. It would take days for a mechanical digger to clear, let alone the three of them with bare hands.

"I don't want to miss Christmas," said Connor. "What can we do?"

"We'll think of something," said Freddie.

Just then, a shrill cry went up from the direction of Ludgate. "There they are! Get them! They're the ones that stole my books! Arrest them!"

In the distance they saw the shrouded man pointing and encouraging four reluctant members of the Watch.

Instinctively Freddie, Connor and Ruby backed away in the direction they had just come from, and the Watch took this as an admission of guilt and started after them.

"Let's run round the outside, and recite 'If—' as we go," said Freddie.

The trio started their homeward mantra, making sure they kept Connor between them. The four Watchmen had a large deficit to make up, but they were gaining.

"Keep going, Conman," encouraged Ruby. The three exhausted friends started the second verse. "If you can dream…" On they ran as they reached the far end of the ruin.

It was more difficult to navigate the southside as the debris was far wider spread, so they had to clamber over hot stones at times. Freddie slipped and Connor grabbed him by the arm to stop him sliding into a pool of molten lead. "Thanks, that was close," he breathed.

Ruby hauled them both over a large stone column that had fallen outwards virtually intact. They turned to see the Watch close behind them. Then came an almighty scream as one of them obviously found the scalding pool Freddie had avoided.

The chase stopped as they pulled the man out, but they came again. All the while the trio continued to chant. As they neared the portal, a purple glow showed itself from within the huge mound of stones. It pulsed and grew stronger with every phrase.

"If you can fill the unforgiving minute…" There was an almighty crack of stones splitting and toppling. Then a blast of flying masonry shot away from the portal in all directions.

Freddie, Connor and Ruby could see inside the vortex. Friendly spirits were tossing debris aside, making way for the returning heroes. But the route was scalding the trio's feet as they picked their way slowly over the last few metres. Connor fell and turned to see that the Watch had stopped dead. They were staring in awe at the huge, shimmering gateway.

But then the shrouded man rose from the top of the heaped stone barring the way to the portal. "Those weren't the diaries. Where are the real ones? I won't let you win, Freddie Malone. You and your pathetic friends won't beat me. I know where you all come from. You will never beat me."

He started flicking molten lead at them from a rock pool with the blade of an abandoned shovel. The boiling liquid spattered around them. Suddenly, a hefty brick-size piece of stone flew through the air and caught the hateful man on the knee. He collapsed in a heap shouting murderous curses. Freddie was sure the way was clear now their enemy was down. The relief flooded through them all, and Freddie hauled Connor upright and finished 'If—' in style.

"Yours is the earth and everything that's in it, And —which is more—you'll be a Man, my son!"

To their left a beautiful horse stood up on its back legs and neighed loudly, as the Dark Rider, his face now entirely masked, dropped a second stone from his hand which was now not needed. He saluted the trio with three distinct jerks of his right hand in an upward arc, and they waved their thanks in return.

Hurrying the last few paces to the portal Freddie shouted, "Find out who the shrouded man is, rip his hood off," and they charged to where he'd fallen. But there was no trace. He'd completely disappeared.

"We'll have to get him next time, eh?" said Connor philosophically, and with one last lingering look at 17th-century London, the trio linked arms and stepped through the portal into the safety of the swirling vortex, which sped them headfirst in the direction of Christmas.

Epilogue

The first chance they all had to be together again was at the Malone's New Year's Eve party. Connor was especially pleased when they were able to retreat, with their loaded plates, to the conservatory – well away from the volatile Finnegan. Then it was on to the business of what to do with Samuel the rat.

"We should get him to a vet, to check he hasn't got fleas. Then we could give him to Mrs Spencer as a class pet," offered Freddie.

Connor nodded. "Yeah! And if she catches the plague from him, it would pay her back for sticking that beard on me in the Pied Piper!"

Freddie laughed.

"But what if he *has* got fleas?" said Ruby. "Samuel will have to be…"

"I guess so. But the vet will know what to do,"

Freddie tried to reassure Ruby. "I don't think he has, though. I spent an hour on Boxing Day checking him over with a magnifying glass. I couldn't see anything moving."

A glum silence overtook them for a few seconds until Connor smiled and said, "Anyone get any good prezzies? Freddie?"

"More socks from Finnegan and Kathleen. I don't know how many feet they think I've got."

All three chuckled. It felt really great to be back together. Stuck in front of the TV for a week with his plankton-like family had been tough for Connor after all the excitement of London. He sat back and said, "I tried to work out what saving a life in 1665 means today." The other two turned with quizzical looks. He continued. "Say, someone we rescued went on to have three children, and all of *them* had three children, in twenty-five years that would be twelve people who wouldn't have existed. In another twenty-five years, another twenty-seven, and after seventy-five years it would be seventy-seven people, making a hundred and sixteen people in seventy-five years. I lost count after that and gave up. But it must be thousands. And we saved twenty kids from St Paul's alone."

"Wow," said Ruby. "Well that explains why London's so crowded!" The three dissolved again into giggles, interrupted by Mrs M who bustled into the conservatory.

"I don't blame you three for hiding in here. But don't forget your antibiotics, Freddie. Last day and the tablets are finished. Now then, Finnegan only wants cheese, so he says. He just shouted at your father that he's *in a lot of pain and never gets the things he wants.*' He's turned into a selfish old..." She restrained herself and hurried back to the lounge with a substantial slab of vintage cheddar, leaving the friends alone again.

"We should practise owl calls, that was a brilliant signal," Ruby said.

"I can bark," said Connor, enthusiastically mimicking an annoying yapping lapdog, and making her spill her drink. Then he pulled his golden guinea from his pocket and the three took turns examining it and reminiscing about the king and the Duke of York.

Freddie hoped his best friend was still on a high from his achievements in London. Connor had been clever, inventive and brave. Freddie was proud of him.

"I hope Billy, Mingoe and Jack do, err, *did,* all the things they said they were going to do," Ruby said, as the others nodded. Freddie felt a rush of affection at the thought of their amazing 17th-century friends. "I bet they did. I don't think anything was going to stop them."

They looked up as Uncle Patrick bounced into the room. "Freddie boy, come on back in and liven up this party! Finnegan's just ruined the atmosphere. Why don't you recite that poem you did on your birthday. I think we need a bit of culture."

"We can *all* do it, if you like," offered Ruby. "Let's do a verse each, and the last one together."

"That'd be grand! And, Connor, are you going to play us a *jig* on that pipe of yours?"

"Sure!"

Freddie smiled, as he saw Connor swell with pride once again.

The party guests were hushed by Patrick and the three made a fantastic job of the poem, encouraging the whole room to join in the famous last line, 'And—which is more—you'll be a Man, my son!'

Cheers and a round of applause followed, and as it started to fade, a simple melody took over, beautifully played by the large boy beside the Christmas tree. His eyes were closed, as through his mind ran the times he'd played this haunting tune in the last two weeks. At the disastrous school play, accompanied by the hissing insults of Casey and the rats. Then in the shopping mall, where the disgusted old lady retrieved her pound coin from the hat. But as the tune built and soared, Connor remembered playing first for Pepys, and then the King of England, and finally, as he led the waifs from the deadly burning crypt to safety.

Connor brimmed with pride and confidence as he bowed grandly at the applause.

Uncle Patrick, ruffled his hair. "That's a precious talent, you've got there, boy. When someone shares their music or a story with you, it's a gift worth more than all the king's gold."

He winked at the trio and handed over three small identical parcels, each wrapped in old newspaper and string. "Don't open them yet, you scallywags! Wait 'til I've gone, and you're away from this bunch of hooligans." He nodded at the crowded room.

And with that, as a rumble of thunder shook the house, he kissed Mrs Malone, slapped his brother on the back and left the festive gathering, striding away in his shorts and Hawaiian shirt into the now pelting rain. Without looking back he saluted: three distinct jerks of his right hand in an upward arc. The friends gasped simultaneously as they watched Uncle Patrick swing out of the gate.

Now they were alone in the hallway, Freddie looked down at his present and carefully unwrapped a small red book. "It's a *diary*. Look! For next year..."

Ruby followed suit and revealed an electric blue

version. "Huh?" she frowned.

After Connor produced a green diary, they all looked at each other silently wondering, their minds whirring...

Then Freddie noticed the paper the books were wrapped in. "This is the *Oxford Gazette*, 2nd of September 1666. Look... It says, 'About two a clock this morning a sudden and lamentable fire broke out in this city...'"

"It's a photocopy, surely... isn't it?" asked Ruby.

"No! No, I think it's real," Freddie replied, rubbing the ancient paper carefully between his fingers.

"Mine's wrapped in a sheet about the plague. Look!" Connor said in a fearful whisper.

"And mine reports the trial of a criminal gang who were found guilty of... I can't believe this!"

Freddie hurriedly opened his diary and almost dropped it as he spotted the first entry inside. There, on January 1st was a coded message in distinctive brown ink. It shone from the page. He struggled to contain his excitement.

"What is it? What does it say?" asked Ruby, urgently.

"It's Pepys's handwriting. I'd know it anywhere." Freddie stared in awe at the symbols.

"Well, what does it say?" echoed Connor frantically.

"It says..." Freddie chuckled. "It says, '*This morning it rained so hard... though it was fair yesterday...*'"

Freddie, Connor and Ruby looked at one another and raced outside into the teeming downpour to see where Patrick had gone. They needed answers, but by the time they got to the pavement, the street was completely deserted.

Freddie's uncle had, quite simply, disappeared.

Author's Notes:
The Facts Behind the Story

Thank you for reading Freddie Malone's third adventure. Hopefully you were as captivated by the history as you were by the story! Some of you may be interested to know what's true and what's not in the pages you've just read.

Let's start with **the plague**. Apart from my inventions of the 'Angels of Mercy', Sir Bradley, the Packers and Billy Jenks, I'm afraid it's all terrifyingly true. If anything, the horrific outbreak was much more gruesome than I have described. The corrupt searchers and watchers were real, as were the gangs who took advantage of the desperate and dying. Cats and dogs were culled, Mayor Lawrence did conduct business from a glass box, and the plague outfits worn by the few doctors who stayed to fight the disease were as described.

William Boghurst was at the forefront of tackling the outbreak, as were the great minds of the newly formed 'Royal Society' (1660). Wigs made from the hair of recent victims were infected and helped spread the disease, but these tresses were about the only things that dropped in price during the plague: everything else quadrupled as people took advantage.

It was a truly terrifying time. The figure of 100,000 deaths is accurate allowing for the corrupt declarations of many searchers. In total, an amazing twenty per cent of the city's population perished.

The crane in St James' Park did have a

Plague doctor costume, showing the beak into which posies were stuffed to mask the stench

wooden leg, although I have exaggerated Pepys's involvement in the provision of its new limb. Pirates were tarred and left in metal cages on the river, Cromwell's head was on a spike at Westminster Hall, and fifteen hundred men and boys disappeared in one week, taken by press gangs as described. Alsatia existed, and was a truly lawless maze where no soldiers or watchmen ever dared enter.

Pepys is a complex figure; an absolute mixture of a man. Undoubtedly clever and fiercely ambitious, he was from much humbler stock than the people he rose to mix with, and was always anxious to impress and improve his station in life. He was not a kind husband and Elizabeth often cuts a sad figure as a result. To his credit, he was very candid in his diaries, which perhaps proves he wasn't trying to leave a sanitised picture of himself for posterity. I still don't know if I'd like him if I met him.

The Great Fire, September 2nd–6th, 1666

I have placed the adventure amongst the actual events, chronology and progress of the fire to the best of my research. The long, hot summer, the tinder-dry wooden houses, the incessant wind fanning the flames westwards until late on the 5th when it turned about and threatened Seething Lane, are all well documented by Pepys, Evelyn,

Samuel Pepys

An extract from Pepys's diary in his unique shorthand

and Taswell. Modern reference works by Tomalin, Mortimer, Bastaple, Porter and Rideal, provide a wonderful framework and context in which to place Freddie.

Pepys's household had been to Bartholomew Fair on the 1st where, for the third time that week, Samuel had been enthralled by the puppet Polichinello and seen the sailor with his dodo.

Mayor Bludworth was desperately at fault for not acting more quickly to create a firebreak whilst still possible and halt the fire as it spread from Thomas Farriner's bread ovens on Pudding Lane. James, Duke of York, did assume command and set up the eight posts from which to fight the blaze. He certainly did get his hands dirty and led by example. Taswell and the Westminster schoolboys did stand shoulder to shoulder against the flames at St Dunstan's, although it is a wishful fantasy of mine that Pepys might have sponsored scholarships to the waifs of St Paul's. Belasyse, De Vere and William Richardson are real, the latter was almost certainly responsible for binding Pepys's diaries at John Cade's shop on Cornhill.

The Tower of London was indeed like a bomb waiting to explode, packed as it was with 600,000 pounds of gunpowder. Some say eighty-five, but more say eighty-seven churches were destroyed as their stone crumbled in the ferocious heat.

The Aftermath

St Paul's was rebuilt by Sir Christopher Wren and although many plans were drawn up, due to insurance and property rights most people rebuilt on the footprint of the land they owned before the fire struck, hence the labyrinth of tight and congested city streets that still exist to this day. Eight people died during the fire, starting with Thomas Farriner's maid, who for fear of falling would not escape along the roof to safety. In a peculiar symmetry to the plague, twenty per cent of the city's buildings were lost.

And last, but certainly not least, **Mingoe and Jack** were indeed slaves to Batten and Penn. However, I have made them 'indentured' so that they can buy themselves the freedom they should never have been denied. The truth is, they were slaves for life. Although Mingoe was left £10 in Batten's will, and £20 a year to maintain the lighthouse at Harwich (a beloved project of Batten's) this was small compensation for an enforced life of servitude.

The slave trade was a despicable chapter in Britain's history that made many individuals and organisations very wealthy. The reference in 'Black lives in the English Archives' that Mingoe and Jack were made to dance by their masters in the Dolphin Tavern disturbed me so much that I wanted to make that event work to their advantage in the story. To used it to empower them. I had to visualise them winning in the end.

It is estimated that over a period of 400 years nearly 13 million Africans were forcibly transported from Central and West Africa, by the Portuguese, British, Spanish, French, Dutch and Danes. Many slaves died on the inhumanly cruel Atlantic voyages, with many more perishing when they arrived in the 'New World'.

In contrast, in order to repay a royal debt of £16,000, Charles II gave Sir William Penn a large parcel of land in the New World, now known as Pennsylvania.

My fantasy of Mingoe and Jack rising to master their own destinies contrasts with the brutal reality of most slaves' experiences. It is my attempt to impress on the reader the colossal importance of the Black Lives Matter movement. Only by studying history and the truly awful mistakes and decisions made by our ancestors can we hope to compensate those innocents who were wronged, and eradicate the chances of similar travesties happening again.

History is important. It is *really* important.

Thanks

Thank you, especially to Carla and Harry, my family, friends and supporters. Everyone at Award Publications, especially Anna and Fiona. My agent Penny Luithlen for her constant support and brilliant advice. The very helpful and knowledgeable staff at the Pepys Library at Magdalene College Cambridge: a glorious way to spend an afternoon.

My thoughts and best wishes are with all those affected by the Covid-19 pandemic and the Black Lives Matter movement of 2020. This book was written in the two years leading up to those events and was meant to be a love letter to London, paying tribute to the lives lost in 1665 and to highlight the plight of all slaves, but it now has a terribly haunting and strange resonance in the time in which we live. I hope the subject matter of this book and the questions raised promote debate and help focus a laser beam of change against injustice in our world, in whatever corner, to whichever people.

Read all the books in the series!

With the help of his best friend, Connor, Freddie embarks on an epic journey through time and space to the Himalayas, and finds himself caught up in a story from mountaineering legend.

Can Freddie and Connor save history – and themselves – in time?

978-1-78270-321-1

978-1-78270-363-1

When Freddie's map sends him back in time to ancient Egypt, he discovers a terrible plot against the boy king, Tutankhamun.

Join Freddie, Connor, and their feisty new neighbour, Ruby, as a dangerous figure threatens to foil their efforts to save the young pharaoh...